WITCHING YOU A CHARMED CHRISTMAS

Jenna Collett

Copyright © 2023 Jenna Collett

All rights reserved

The characters and events portrayed in this book are fictitious. Any similarity to real persons, living or dead, is coincidental and not intended by the author.

No part of this book may be reproduced, or stored in a retrieval system, or transmitted in any form or by any means, electronic, mechanical, photocopying, recording, or otherwise, without express written permission of the publisher.

ISBN: 9798871338414
Imprint: Independently published

V1
Printed in the United States of America

CONTENTS

Title Page
Copyright
Note to Reader
Chapter 1   1
Chapter 2   11
Chapter 3   19
Chapter 4   26
Chapter 5   31
Chapter 6   40
Chapter 7   47
Chapter 8   55
Chapter 9   65
Chapter 10   74
Chapter 11   82
Chapter 12   91
Chapter 13   99
Chapter 14   105

Chapter 15	115
Books By This Author	125

NOTE TO READER

Dear reader,

I'm so excited for you to read this story!

A little hint about what you'll be getting inside these pages:

If you like your Christmas stories sweet, with some steamy kisses, loads of witty banter, a hero with a Scrooge complex, and a witchy heroine who's out to grant him a Christmas miracle, then I hope you enjoy this magical holiday novella.

Happy Reading,

Jenna Collett

CHAPTER 1
Delia

—Three Weeks Until Christmas—

The gingerbread cookie looked more like a zombie than a man. Its limbs were bent at awkward angles, and its head was smashed in on one side. I wrinkled my nose at my lackluster baking skills and added an extra glob of white icing, then sliced off the lumpy head between my teeth.

With zombies, you always aim for the head, and when life gets you down, you add extra sugar. Considering it was the start of December, and I was still single and sitting at the bottom of the witchy corporate ladder at my job, I squeezed a dollop of icing straight into my mouth and chased it with a long sip from my white wine spritzer.

"Stupid fortune teller," I muttered as I reached for another ghastly cookie. "That's the last time I get life advice from a mystic."

Though to be fair, Madam Destiny was the most respected psychic around. She had a waiting list a mile long, and her visions practically came with a guarantee. When she'd claimed by the end of the year, I'd be promoted to agent and that Simon Delacour, my long-time office crush was actually *the one* and I'd finally capture his attention, I was thrilled.

But then just last week, I was passed over for the job—again—and Simon barely knew I existed.

I cringed, imagining the not-so-festive weeks in front of me. Another holiday of pitying looks, "you'll get em next time" shoulder bumps, and lame attempts to shove me under the mistletoe at the upcoming office Christmas party.

Off came another gingerbread head.

The headless cookie in my hand was starting to look appealing. *Can you show up to a Christmas party with a gingerbread man for a date?* I could ice him a suit and cast an animation spell. Desperate times called for desperate measures.

But it was probably a bad idea. Everyone would think he was my sugar daddy.

I snorted into my wine, laughing at my own joke. Rock-bottom, meet my absurd and highly underappreciated sense of humor.

The cookies were nearly gone, and tv was heading into late-night infomercial territory when I kicked the blanket off my legs and poured myself into bed. An intermittent buzz dared to drag me from my sleep, and I grabbed my phone from the bedside table.

"If you called to tell me how amazing your ski vacation is, I'll take a hard pass. It's late, and I'm grieving a lifetime of mediocrity while trying to slip into a sugar coma," I grumbled into the phone.

My best friend and coworker at the agency, Sage, made a tsking sound and asked, "Cake or candy?"

"Neither. Cookies. I baked an army of gingerbread men and then ate their heads in protest."

"Savage. Those were innocent victims."

I pressed a hand against my stomach as it rumbled and twisted from too much flour and sugar. "My developing heartburn says otherwise. But I'm awake now, so you might as well tell me, how are the mountains?"

Sage hesitated. "That's why I'm calling. There's a bit of an issue. It's a long story that involves an avalanche that might—sort of—be my fault, and thanks to my magical mishap, I'm stuck inside a remote ski village for the foreseeable future."

"How was an avalanche your fault?"

"That's not important. What's important is I need a huge favor. I'm supposed to work on my next case this week, but since I'm trapped in a winter-not-so-wonderland, I want you to cover for me. Upper management already cleared the case transfer, and the research is done. All you have to do is read the case file, work a little magic, and deliver a Christmas miracle! Easy peasy."

I rolled upright and clutched the phone tighter, the breath catching in the back of my throat. "Upper management is going to let me take a case?"

"I put in a good word for you. It's a trial run, but completing this job will put you in line for a promotion. Christmas miracles are the gold standard at the agency. You'll be a shoo-in. Plus..." Sage paused for effect. "The office next to Simon's is currently vacant. It could be yours in a matter of weeks. He'll definitely take notice of you then. First, you'll share a wall, then a meal. Next thing you know, you'll be sharing a penthouse overlooking the harbor."

I squeezed my eyes shut and fist-pumped the air. *Don't ever discredit a fortune teller, especially one named Madam Destiny.*

"You're the best Sage. I've never been so happy for an avalanche."

Sage groaned. "Well, I'm glad someone's happy. I'm the one snowed in. Go into the office on Monday and collect my case file. You won't be sorry, and we can celebrate your new office and future boyfriend when I get back. Oh, and Del?"

"Yeah?"

"Try not to murder any more gingerbread men."

I stifled a grin. "Deal."

***

A blast of icy air slid under my scarf as I hurried toward the steel and glass tower of my office building. From the outside looking in, we sold antique novelties, but we really granted wishes, broke curses, and performed miracles.

Our Holidays Division, Christmas specifically, was our busiest branch composed of our best agents. I'd started a few years ago in a different division and had worked my way up to Holidays. Now if I could score an agent's promotion, I'd finally be living my dream.

Agents got to work in the field, helping people and bettering their lives, while I was currently stuck in the office documenting case outcomes and performing basic administrative tasks. If someone needed paperclips or there was an odd smell coming from the break room refrigerator, they called me. And we were witches, so some smells coming from that thing were vile.

Nodding at the young woman working the reception desk, I weaved through the cubicle jungle with a spring in my step. The spring faltered when my cube mate Agatha popped her perfectly coifed head above the half wall separating our spaces. Her cherry-red lips smacked together and formed a sickly sweet smile.

"Delia! You're *finally* here. There's a whole cart of poinsettias that needs to be delivered to each agent's office. I'd do it myself, but I just had my nails done. I'd hate to chip the paint." She wriggled her inch-long, red and green sparkly nails in front of her nose. "Besides, you're never busy with anything important."

"Actually, Agatha, I've been assigned a case. I need to brush up on the file this morning."

Agatha wrinkled her nose. "They never assign cases to low-level witches. Don't lie to get out of plant duty." With a smug look, she reached for a pair of earbuds, popped them into her ears, and focused her attention on her laptop. The muffled melodies of Christmas music filled the cube as Agatha iced me out.

"I won't be low-level for long," I muttered while unwinding my scarf and shrugging out of my coat. I dropped my bag and looked longingly at my laptop before heaving a sigh and heading toward the poinsettias. The case could wait a few minutes while I unloaded the cart.

Vibrant red leaves greeted me, and I brushed off Agatha's snarky attitude. Things were looking up. I finally had a case of my own. This would be my last time passing out holiday decorations. Next season, I'd be the one receiving them.

I pushed the cart forward, frowning when it wouldn't budge. Shoving harder only made it shuddered a few inches, and nearly toppled a plant onto the carpet. I rebalanced the poinsettia, checked to make sure the wheels weren't stuck, and then leaned all my weight into the cart.

Little-by-little, I made my way down the hall, delivering potted poinsettias to lucky agents. A sheen of sweat made my silk blouse stick to my skin, and I blew a wayward strand of hair out of my face as I shoved the cart as hard as I could, trying to reach the last office.

The cart bucked, loosening a wheel and sending it rolling through the open doorway. I peeked inside the dimly lit office. Of course, it was Simon's, and I breathed in the faint, lingering scent of his expensive cologne. His office was sparsely decorated with a mahogany desk and a set of sleek black leather chairs. A bookcase lined one wall, and the other was dotted with framed certificates. But the pièce de résistance was the giant window overlooking the city. The view from this side of the building was incredible, especially in the evening when the sun dipped below the skyline and the city lights twinkled.

Looking over my shoulder to make sure the coast was clear, I tip-toed inside Simon's office to search for the missing wheel. The blasted thing had rolled underneath his desk, forcing me to contort my body to reach it.

"Looking for something?" Simon's deep baritone sent a shock through my body, and I nearly rammed my head into a drawer.

The tips of my fingers snagged the wheel, and I shimmied out from beneath the desk. I held up the wheel while sheepishly smoothing the edge of my skirt.

"Sorry. I was delivering the poinsettias, and the cart revolted. Let me get yours." The back of my neck heated as I scrambled past Simon and snagged the last potted plant. I inhaled a calming breath and whirled to find him standing behind me.

Simon's mouth curled into a sexy grin. "You're Sage's friend, right? Something that starts with a D? I always see you around the office."

"D—Delia, Delia Frost," I stammered, holding out the plant while trying not to squeal with the knowledge he knew my name. *Sort of.* Starts with a D should count.

He waved away the poinsettia, and his smile deepened, crinkling his blue eyes. "Congrats on getting your first case. I just heard this morning." He winked. "Take my plant. You might need it to decorate your new office."

I tucked the poinsettia against my chest, my heart pounding. It was happening! Things were falling into place faster than snowflakes during a blizzard.

"Um, thanks..." My tongue twisted and my brain screamed—*"Don't mention the fortuneteller or the gingerbread massacre. Keep the fact that he smells like a holiday-spiced candle to yourself."*

But say something!

When I remained woefully silent, Simon leaned forward and plucked the wheel from my fingers.

"Let me help you with that, Dhalia."

Wait… My brow creased.

"It's Delia," I murmured, but he wasn't paying attention.

Simon bent and placed the wheel near the cart, then with a flick of magic, he reattached it. Lifting the edge of the cart, he spun the wheel easily.

"All fixed. I guess I'll be seeing you more often if we're going to be office mates. Hey, maybe we can even grab lunch sometime."

Simon flashed me his teeth and strode down the hall, leaving me hugging the poinsettia. *Cloud Nine here I come.* We were going to grab lunch—sometime.

I wheeled the cart smoothly toward the supply closet, then practically floated back to my desk. Nothing could burst this moment. Not even Simon's lousy memory when it came to my name. He'd gifted me with his holiday plant. The gorgeous red leaves brightened my postage stamp-sized cube—without a window or any semblance of a view.

Agatha pulled an earbud from her ear. "Where did you get those? I hope you didn't steal them from the cart. They're for the agents."

I rubbed a velvety leaf between my thumb and forefinger and shrugged. "Simon gave them to me. He's so thoughtful."

Agatha snorted and tapped out a few words on her laptop. "I think you mean he's so allergic. He chucks them in the bin every year."

My shoulders slumped. Would he have thrown them away? I flipped open my laptop, shaking off my disappointment, and opened my email. I located one from Sage containing the details of my case. Things were different now, and I refused to let Agatha get to me. Maybe Simon threw out his poinsettia every year, but not this year. This year, he gave it to me.

It was symbolic.

A sign.

An early Christmas gift from the universe, and I wasn't one to turn away a gift.

Ignoring Agatha's negativity, I double-clicked on the email from Sage and opened the case file. My eyes widened at the target's profile photo. A buzzing in my ears drowned out the office noise.

"Well, hello, Jack Bradley," I murmured under my breath.

The photo was candid and taken while he stood among an overgrown patch of pine trees. Wearing a blue checkered flannel shirt, dark jeans, and black work boots, he appeared at home in his surroundings. The wind tousled his raven-black hair, and his sturdy hands gripped an axe, resting it against one of his broad shoulders.

There wasn't a casualness in his stance, and his face seemed set in stone. His stubble-covered jaw was clenched in a frown, lips flat as if the pine trees had done him wrong and were about to meet their maker. But his eyes told a different story. There was a vulnerability there. Some raw emotion bound tightly beneath his rugged frame.

He looked like he needed to laugh, but also as if any hint of a joke might send his axe swinging.

My gaze dropped from Jack's photo to his detailed brief. He lived in the small town of Wood Pine and owned an inn and a derelict Christmas tree farm that had both seen better days.

The case file disclosed the task. Apparently, Jack had a Scrooge complex, and the town avoided him like the plague, especially during the holiday season. He was anti-love and hadn't dated in years. Which was the real tragedy in this file considering the way he looked in flannel.

Unfortunately, the Scrooge complex would be tricky. I could see why solving this case might earn me a promotion. Changing a grumpy attitude like that usually took ghosts. But I didn't have ghosts. I had a bunch of magic spells, an urgent desire to finally prove myself career-wise, and the hope of becoming Simon's girlfriend by the new year.

Totally doable, even without the spooky spirits.

There was a timeframe listed on the case, and Sage had circled the date in red, writing "critical" beneath the deadline.

As his case agent, I needed to help Jack find love and heal his emotional wounds surrounding the holiday before midnight on Christmas Eve.

By the looks of it, he needed a miracle. Lucky for both of us, I was in the business of granting them.

CHAPTER 2
Jack

The hand saw bit into the tree trunk, shuddering as I dragged it through the bark. Needing a better angle, I hunkered low to the ground, gritting my teeth as an icy slush soaked through my pants. One of these days, I'd remember to grab the tarp lying in the shed. But wet clothes and freezing weather weren't my only problem. Prickly pine needles jabbed me in the face, and I sucked in a frozen breath, hoping a few more cuts would send the tree crashing into the snow.

How many trees did I have to sell to make a profit this year? *Way too many.* To make matters worse, business was slow. No, make that almost non-existent. My only customer today was a man who'd waved away the saw, along with the alleged charm of cutting his own tree, and told me to just get one and bring it out. He was texting on his phone before I even turned around.

Fine. Miss out on the memories. What do I care? It's your overblown holiday.

With a creak and a whoosh, the tree collapsed in defeat, deflating into a pile of bristled branches. Sweat cooled against my neck, and I wiped the sleeve of my jacket over my brow. The tree in question was gangly, and not fit to grace a living room, but I needed it sold, or I'd be living under one like it soon enough.

I wrapped the uneven branches in twine and hauled the tree through the thin layer of snow back to the man's vehicle.

"That'll be a hundred bucks," I said, dropping the trunk at the customer's feet.

The man eyed the sorry excuse for a Christmas tree and shook his head. "For that shabby tree? I'll give you fifteen dollars, and you can tie it to the roof of my car for free. Take it or leave it."

I ground my molars. I wasn't in the position to leave it, and he knew it. The whole town knew it. You didn't drive out to my farm to find a gem. There were no diamonds in this rough, just a town outcast trying to unload a bunch of wretched trees before they nailed a foreclosed sign into the gate.

"Fine. I'll take it." I pocketed the pitiful sum, then heaved the tree onto the car's roof and tied it down. Pine needles fluttered to the ground, dusting the snow with green flecks.

Good riddance. One tree down, another acre's worth to go.

The man smirked and waved his hand through the car window as he peeled out of the lot. "Merry Christmas!"

"Don't come back next year!" I shouted at his tail lights.

Though, at this rate, there wouldn't be a farm to come to next year. Guilt shredded my insides. If my father could see this place now… I forced away another spear of guilt. He never should have left me the family business. Who knows why he did? It was probably a clerical error or his idea of punishment. It certainly was one of mine.

I grabbed the saw and trudged toward the small inn at the end of the drive. The four guestroom cottage still held its charm, even though it badly needed paint and a few noticeable repairs. From its gabled roof, adorned with white ornate trim, and a layer of glistening snow, to the cozy front porch with detailed wood columns, the house had always been a seasonal treasure. In days past, the front door had boasted a giant wreath and garlands hung in every window.

But all the decorations were still boxed deep in the attic, along with the tangled mess of string lights my father had used to cover every inch of the property. For years, the farm had been bustling with families looking for the perfect tree while guests sipped cocoa outside by the massive stone fire pit.

Until that night...

A shudder shook my frame, and I shoved the dark memory from my mind. This was my lot now. An empty, rundown inn and a pathetic tree farm. No sense in remembering better days. Christmas was for fools and anyone trying to convince me otherwise could go face-plant in a snowbank.

The crunch of ice beneath tires caught my attention, and I steeled myself for another customer. My fingers clenched around the saw, and when I turned, I wasn't prepared for what greeted me.

A young woman stepped out of a taxi, and then

promptly slipped on a patch of ice, catching herself on the door of the car. A giant rolling suitcase wasn't so lucky and tumbled to her feet. With a shake of her head, she dusted the snow off her suitcase, grabbed a potted plant from the back seat, and then waved cheerily at the driver as if she hadn't almost nosedived into the driveway.

Brown knee-high boots with dangerously narrow heels clung to her legging-covered calves, and an off-white sweater dress peeked beneath a long coat lined with light gray fur. She tossed her dark glossy hair over her shoulder to reveal a pair of dangling candy cane earrings and a matching choker. The woman bent to pull her suitcase, tucked the plant under her arm, and carefully shuffled across the slushy drive toward me.

"You could use a little road salt back there."

My gaze dropped to her boots. Not only were they ill-suited for ice, but they didn't look warm. Her feet were probably freezing. The irrational thought soured my mood further. "Or you could wear proper footwear. This isn't a fashion runway, it's a farm. You're going to break your neck."

Seemingly oblivious to my surly tone, she shrugged. "Like I said, nothing a little road salt couldn't fix, or a bag of sand. It's good business practice to keep your roads clear of ice. But that answers my next question. This must be the Bradley Inn. I have a reservation."

Her smile was as blinding as the sun on freshly fallen snow, and I almost shaded my eyes to dim the effect. Lips the color of warm cranberries drew my interest, and the way the cold tinted her cheeks made something stir inside my chest.

I scowled. *Nope.* This pixie sprite of holiday nonsense and best business practices was NOT staying here.

"Sorry. We're completely booked. You'll have to try the hotel in town."

The wind swirled the ends of her hair as she peered at the inn behind me. She gestured toward a wooden sign hanging on a chain. "The sign over there says vacancy, and the woman I spoke to on the phone last night told me I'd have the place to myself. She said I was the first guest in weeks. With no other reservations in sight."

My eyes narrowed into slits. *Grandma Jean strikes again.* I was taking her off phone duty.

Between gritted teeth, I said, "My mistake. Welcome to our Inn. I'll let my grandmother know you're here so she can show you to your room."

Her brow rose as she studied the object gripped tightly in my hand. "Do you always greet your guests wielding a saw? With the tree farm and the gingerbread house backdrop, you're kind of giving off serial killer Santa vibes."

"Make sure to leave that in your review," I deadpanned, pointing the saw blade toward the inn, punctuating her point. "After you."

"Delia. My name's Delia Frost. It's nice to meet you…" She paused, waiting for me to introduce myself.

"Jack," I replied gruffly, reaching for her suitcase. "Jack, the Kringle Killer. Let's go. I have trees to slay."

A musical laugh burst from her throat as she fell into step beside me. She nudged me in the arm. "Santa sleigh

15

pun intended, am I right?"

The corner of my mouth twitched, and I bit down hard on my cheek. What was I doing? The woman barely reached my shoulders like some kind of woodland elf, and she smelled like vanilla icing. She was trouble draped in tinsel, and I was finding her another place to stay as soon as possible.

I'd make up a story. Burst plumbing. A heater on the fritz. If I had to cut the power at the breaker panel, I would. With a flip of a switch, she'd leave, and I wouldn't have to bother hanging holiday lights around the inn. Dark and alone, just the way I liked it. Win-win.

When we reached the front door, it swung open on a rusty hinge, and my grandmother threw out her arms. We might not have had any recent guests, but this welcome was overkill.

"You made it!" she cheered like they were long-lost friends. "Right on time. Please, call me Grandma Jean, everyone does. I have your room all ready. It's the best one we have, with a beautiful view of the tree farm."

"Grandma, you didn't tell me we booked a guest. How long is she staying?"

"Till Christmas!" Delia piped in, following my grandmother into the common room. "Grandma Jean, this place is lovely."

My brow creased. Were we seeing the same room? The hearth was filled with soot, sitting beneath a mantel bare of decorations. A lone pine tree sat in the corner, slightly bent—unsurprising since it came from out back—and lacking ornaments. This room was devoid of joy on purpose.

"Ah, it could use a little cheer. I keep begging my grandson to pull down the decorations from the attic. But he's so busy. Running a farm like this is exhausting, and we've had trouble finding help this year."

"Well, your grandson definitely knows how to brandish a saw. It wasn't menacing at all," Delia said with a suppressed grin. "But don't do anything extra on my account. You won't even know I'm here."

I clenched my jaw. *Unlikely. But it won't matter, you're not staying.*

Grandma Jean clapped her hands together. "Let me show you upstairs and get you settled. Here's your key." She handed Delia a long brass key with a red tassel hanging from the end.

I watched Delia head for the stairs, realizing I still had her suitcase. I was not a bellboy, but then again, she'd probably topple down the staircase in those heels if she tried to bring it up to her room.

With a heavy sigh and an internal pep talk that I would be loading said suitcase into the back of a taxi in no time, I delivered the luggage to her door.

Delia popped her head out of the room as my grandmother droned on about the tricky hot water in the bathroom and the perks of fresh cookies in the afternoon. *News to me, I've never seen any cookies.*

She grabbed her suitcase and sent me a wink. "Catch ya later, killer. Don't forget that road salt."

The door closed in my face, and I blinked at her dismissal. Three weeks till Christmas.

Three. Long. Weeks.

There was no way I was sharing this house with that

woman. Meals were out of the question.

My grandmother and I had already decided to sell the inn at the start of the new year, and she'd also agreed to no guests. I had a farm to run—into the ground—and a dreaded holiday to hibernate through. If I wanted peace and quiet till the end, that was my business. I didn't need any distractions or temptations.

What I needed was a plan.

A sly grin spread across my face. Delia Frost wouldn't last the night.

CHAPTER 3
Delia

Grandma Jean pressed her ear against the bedroom door and waited until Jack's footsteps faded down the stairs. "I think he's gone. We can talk freely now. I'm grateful the agency sent someone so quickly. I heard there was a waiting list."

I hefted my suitcase onto the bed and placed my plant on the nightstand, before turning to the older woman. Her fine gray hair was trimmed short with soft layers, and she wore a cozy green cable-knit sweater with loose slacks. Around her neck hung an amethyst on a chain; the occult symbol for calmness and serenity. It suited her. While her grandson seemed consumed by a dark cloud, Grandma Jean was pure light.

"I'm happy to be here. We have a stellar record at the agency, and our division tries to handle as many cases as we can each holiday. Though, I have to ask since often we work undercover, how did you hear about us?"

Grandma Jean pressed her fingers around the amethyst and gave me a knowing look. "I'm the founder of the town's Spells and Brews Ladies' Club. It's a small group, and none of us have actual magical powers, but we do craft a mean Winter's Moon spiced cider. It's wonderful for stomach upsets and pleasant dreams."

"Sounds delicious."

"It is! Anyway, as I was saying, nothing has seemed to help my grandson's disposition. He's had such a difficult time after a broken engagement, and a falling out with his father. I don't know the things that were said, but Jack walked away from everything and didn't return to Wood Pine until after his father's death last year—at Christmastime, of course. It's been downhill ever since. Drastic measures were needed, so I put out some feelers, and through word of mouth, I received a business card. After I sent in my letter, I crossed my fingers."

"Well, it's nice to have an ally. This is my first official Scrooge case." It was my first case altogether, but she didn't need to know that.

Grandma Jean laughed. "It's that bad, isn't it? Jack could give Ebenezer a run for his money. He hates this holiday through and through. If he even suspects you're trying to change his mind, he'll revolt and make your life miserable. I wasn't supposed to allow any guests this season, so there's already a mark against you."

I waved her away with an eye roll and tapped the top of my suitcase containing my mystical bag of tricks. "Don't worry about me. I can handle anything Jack throws my way. Plus, I have a game plan. Your grandson won't even know what hit him. When we're through, he'll be a Christmas convert. It's our agency guarantee."

"You'll have your hands full for sure. But if you need anything, let me know. I'll let you settle in. Dinner's at six. I hope you like meatloaf."

"I do, and if you're up to it, I'd love to try a little of that spiced cider."

"I'd be honored to make some." Grandma Jean slipped through the door, shutting it softly behind her.

Once alone, I let out a tired groan and collapsed onto the bed. Nerves and excitement churned in my stomach, and I wasn't kidding about the spiced cider. Magic potion or not, I needed all the help I could get.

Jack was exactly what his file had depicted, yet at the same time, he was so much more. Sure, he did his photo justice, looking like he'd stepped out of a rugged outdoorsmen catalog, but he also had a dry sense of humor that I found appealing. Somewhere under all that bluster and cynicism was the true Jack. The one that existed before misfortune and tragedy got in the way.

It was my job to heal those wounds, and nothing mended a scarred heart like newfound love. It could breathe life into even the coldest soul. Thankfully, my case file already contained the perfect candidate.

Not everyone in town avoided Jack like he was a radioactive snowman. There was one hopeful contender for Jack's heart: the sweet, but shy local pastry chef, who also harbored a tiny crush. At least she used to. Considering Jack's dismal disposition, I might need to fan the flames—or light the match all over again. Whatever it took. I planned to melt Jack's icy heart one way or another.

Professionally. Of course.

It shouldn't be too hard. I had a bunch of classic meet cutes and magical romantic entanglements to cast their way. There was a formula for this type of thing. Throw in a witchy matchmaker and it was a sure bet.

Let him try to stop me.

***

After dinner and a long hot bath, I settled in for the night in front of my laptop. Next to me was a cup of spiced cider and a small fruit and cheese plate Grandma Jean must have delivered while I was in the bathroom. I popped a grape into my mouth and clicked open Jack's file. He hadn't graced our presence for dinner, but that was fine. It gave me a chance to visit with Grandma Jean. She filled me in a little more about their situation, and we discussed the best way to lure Jack into town.

The local bakery wasn't open until the day after tomorrow, so I had some time to kill. But it would be nice to explore the grounds and have a chance to study my grumpy subject and learn his quirks.

I stretched the kinks from my neck and whipped off an email to Sage, letting her know I'd arrived. Darkness had settled over the farm, and with it came a kind of quiet I wasn't used to. It was almost *too* quiet…and *cold.* I shivered and slid the computer off my lap, searching the room for the source of the chill. Was the heater broken? It hadn't been this bad when I checked in.

The room itself was cozy with extra blankets folded at the edge of the bed and thick drapes hanging in front of a sliding glass door. But that was where the chilly air was coming from. I shuffled across the room and pushed back the curtains. The balcony door was wide open, and a huge blast of icy air hit me in the face.

Winter tears stung the corners of my eyes as I stepped outside onto the balcony and peered into the dark yard. There were no lights, and I could just make out the faint silhouettes of trees dotting the landscape. Nothing moved. The night seemed peaceful and still. But suspicion tingled the back of my neck.

The sliding door had not been open when I went down for dinner. I shoved it closed, using all my upper body strength to force it back into place. That would have been the end of it, except my gaze landed on the floor, catching sight of a muddy boot print. A man's size eleven, at least. Unless the inn was haunted by a mischievous ghost I could wrangle into reenacting scenes from A Christmas Carol, the boot print had to be Jack's.

According to Grandma Jean, Jack had wanted to close the inn early for the season, preferring to keep the house empty and devoid of tradition. But if that man thought he could send me packing from a little chill in the air, then he was sorely mistaken. I'd sleep wearing a hat and mittens if it meant getting this promotion. I'd wear long johns and build myself a blanket fort. I'd—

Something rustled in the corner by the closet.

A chill that had nothing to do with the night air, climbed up my spine. I inched toward the sound, keeping my eyes trained on the mound of extra pillows sitting on top of a cedar chest. They were moving which wasn't a good sign. Was it a bird? Maybe a mouse? I stifled a shudder. *If this place is infested with mice...*

But no. An opossum with a furry gray head and a white snout popped up between the pillows and froze, staring at me with beady eyes. It had a thin hairless tail and pointed ears, along with a cute pink nose. The little guy had probably crept in from the balcony to find a warm place to rest. I couldn't blame him, considering how cold the night air was. Thankfully, opossums were shy, docile creatures, and this one was probably more scared of me than I was of it.

But that didn't mean I was willing to share my room. Cute nose or not, the little guy had to go. I raised my hands in front of me as if the act could somehow calm the critter long enough for me to come up with a plan. It wasn't like I had a cage handy or even a broom to nudge him toward the balcony.

"Hey there, buddy," I crooned. "It's all right. Why don't we go back outside?"

The opossum cocked its head and inched to the edge of the cedar chest. *See, he's listening. This isn't so bad.* His tail arched, and I hesitated. Had I moved too fast?

"Want a piece of fruit, little guy? I have a whole yummy plate over there." I wriggled my fingers, casting a quick spell to waft the scent of sliced apples and oranges in his direction.

The critter's eyes darted to the fruit plate. He sniffed the air but wasn't fooled by my attempt to put him back outside. His mouth opened, revealing at least fifty sharp, pointed teeth. *Okay... not so cute anymore or as shy as I'd like.* When the creature let out a terrifying hiss, I yelped and lunged for the door. I whipped it open, then slammed it closed, leaning heavily against the wood. My eyes squeezed shut as I imagined the hissing animal ravaging the fruit plate, then crawling into my suitcase to burrow inside my sweaters for a long winter's nap.

I blew out a breath. I needed to relax. It was just an opossum. Although nightmarish, his hiss was worse than his bite. At least I was pretty sure opossums didn't bite. Either way, survival odds were in my favor, and there was no way I was letting Jack-the-grumpy-innkeeper take care of the situation he'd likely created in the first place. I'd rather go toe to toe with Mother Nature and lose.

There was no other choice. If snacks didn't lure the critter, maybe I could cast some sort of wildlife coercion spell. It had worked for the Pied Piper! Though it might wake every animal in the vicinity. I didn't want to be their leader, I just didn't want to share a room with anything that had a tail.

The sound of soft laughter made me freeze, and I cringed, recognizing Jack's low tone. Of course, he was lurking in the shadows, likely hoping I'd run screaming down the stairs and all the way back to town. The troublemaker leaned against the stair rail, boots crossed at the ankles, arms folded over his flannel-covered chest. His smirk could have won an award for World's Most Infuriating Facial Feature. Second runner-up to the gleam of victory in his eyes.

"Going somewhere, Delia?" he asked.

CHAPTER 4
Jack

Wildlife invasion for the win.

I never imagined forgetting to remove the animal's nest on the second-floor balcony would prove to be so useful. But the cherry on my sabotage sundae was delivering Delia a late-night snack under the guise of a welcoming host. Was it my fault opossums loved fruit? Sure, I may have left a trail of berries leading toward the open door, but it's not like I picked the critter up and brought him inside.

That was just good fortune.

Some would even call it karma.

"Is there a problem with your room?" I asked with an innocent tilt of my head.

Delia's eyes narrowed. "Strangely enough, there is. Someone opened my balcony door while I was in the bathroom, and now I have an unwanted guest."

"Oops." I shrugged and pushed off the stair rail, doing everything in my power to keep a straight face. "That's my fault. After our shaky start, I wanted to make up for it with a complimentary fruit plate. I knocked, but no one answered. Your do not disturb sign wasn't up, so I figured I'd just leave it on your table. But then I noticed the room smelled musty, so I tried to air it out for you. Top-notch housekeeping is part of our charm."

"Sure it is," Delia muttered, wincing when something crashed inside the room. She braved a look by opening the door a few inches. I peered over her shoulder, biting the inside of my cheek at the mess. In a matter of minutes, the opossum had scampered around the room wreaking havoc. Pillows were strewn across the floor and the fruit plate had been pillaged, leaving grapes, nuts, and half-eaten cheese on the bedspread. Delia's poinsettia hadn't fared well either. The festive shrub was the victim of the muffled crash we'd heard.

"I hope you weren't attached to that plant."

"Oh no, not Simon!"

Delia gasped when she located her poinsettia in a pile of dirt by the nightstand. She rushed into the room, ignoring the pesky opossum who'd decided to play dead and was currently lying prone on the floor. Delia knelt next to the fallen plant and carefully turned it upright, groaning as a leaf came loose.

Simon? I made a face. "You name your plants?"

Her head shot up as she tucked the poinsettia against her chest. "Not usually, but this one is special. It was a gift. You know, an object given to show thoughtfulness and caring." Her lips curled with sarcasm. "Or maybe you don't know anything about the act of brightening someone's day."

Her barb hit home with more force than I thought possible. It must have registered on my face because her features softened, but she didn't apologize. Instead, she dipped her head and tried to scoop dirt back into the foil-wrapped pot. When she'd gotten most of it, she stood with renewed determination, bolstered by a surprisingly cute scowl. Delia walked a wide circle around the sprawled critter, grabbed her suitcase, and started throwing everything inside.

She was leaving. Finally. I waited for the rush of relief, but it never came. It would though, once I'd regained my solitude. This place would stop smelling like sugar cookies, and I wouldn't have to listen to her hum Christmas carols while she helped my grandmother dry the dishes. Not that I was eavesdropping. I just happened to be walking past the kitchen after Operation Opossum Bait.

"I'll call you a taxi. The hotel downtown should have a vacancy."

Delia zipped her suitcase and offered me a grateful smile. It was warmer than I deserved and somehow seemed to sear itself in my mind. Along with the enticing image of her wearing a button-down green pajama top that clung to her curves, and a pair of candy cane stripped bottoms. A matching set of fuzzy slippers covered her feet.

"Thank you, but I won't be needing the taxi." She plucked her battered plant off the nightstand and wheeled her suitcase out of the room. I stood there stunned by her abrupt departure before I lurched after her down the hall. The image of her wearing cozy sleepwear was replaced with her wandering the icy road at night in the same pajamas, and I barely had the forethought to shut the opossum inside the room before she turned the corner.

"You can't go outside like that! It's five miles to town in freezing temperatures." And I had *not* put rock salt on the drive like she'd suggested. Delia might not be wearing heels this time, but fuzzy slippers weren't known for their traction. She wouldn't even make it to the main road!

Delia slowed to a stop. "Your concern is noted, but unnecessary."

"It's not concern. It's common sense!"

There was that smile again, but this time it was like she knew a secret. With a quick turn of the doorknob, and a slight kick from a fuzzy slipper, she stepped inside the darkened room behind her.

"I don't need a taxi because I'm not leaving. I'm switching rooms. Good night, Jack. I trust you'll take care of our little infestation." Delia winked, then slammed the door in my face and twisted the deadbolt.

What. Just. Happened?

A light appeared beneath the gap in the door, and Delia started humming another holiday jingle as she presumably unpacked her suitcase. She was probably crooning to her stupid poinsettia, gently arranging the leaves of her special gift. *Simon, ugh.* What a ridiculous name for a plant. Her words pricked my armor again. How dare she accuse me of not knowing how to brighten someone's day?

I could do a heck of a lot better than a lame seasonal shrub that was about five bucks a pop at the local big box store. If that was a gift from her boyfriend, then she needed to up her standards. Seeing how desperate she was to save the blasted thing made me think I was right.

My teeth ground together. Whether Delia had a boyfriend who failed at gift-giving shouldn't matter. What mattered was my plan had failed. And now I needed a new one, or I'd be stuck with the Candy Cane Princess until Christmas. I scraped a hand through my hair, exhaustion weighing heavy on my shoulders.

How I'd become embroiled in this nonsense was beyond me! I was supposed to be counting down the days to ditching the farm and planning my escape, but instead, I was planning retaliation.

Trudging back to free my furry accomplice, I cycled through a few ideas. Wild animals were out and so were any more trojan horse fruit plates. Cutting the heat might make sleeping painfully cold, but in a win for Delia, her new room had a working fireplace and enough kindling to last the night.

No. It had to be something she couldn't fix herself. An idea formed and with it came a jolt of satisfaction. Delia's current room might be equipped with a fireplace, but Grandma Jean had been in the middle of overhauling the furnishings, most notably, removing the broken blinds.

Time to show Delia just how much I could brighten her day—well, make that night.

CHAPTER 5
Delia

It was well after midnight, and I'd only gotten a few moments of fitful sleep since I'd switched rooms. At this rate, the bags under my eyes wouldn't fit in an airplane's overhead bin. Every time I tried to sleep, I pictured the confident gleam in Jack's eyes or his disapproval when he assumed I planned to walk into town in the middle of the night. As if I'd really parade through Wood Pine in my pajamas. But the worst expression, the one that seemed to stick like molten molasses in my mind was the scorching look he'd given me while I packed my suitcase.

I had not imagined it, even though anything heated coming from Jack had to be a fluke or maybe a medical emergency. But that had not stopped the air from lodging in my throat as his gaze traveled from my messy ponytail, all the way down to my fuzzy slippers. *And wow... talk about toe-curling.* His gaze had lingered longer than a witch at a Black Friday potion sale. Not even the opossum playing dead a few feet away could have broken that spell.

A laugh rumbled inside my chest as I fluffed the pillow behind my head and turned on my side to face the giant picture window. Bruised poinsettias, demolished charcuterie boards, and feral opossums were not romantic trimmings in my book. So what if Jack had shown me more interest in thirty seconds than Simon had shown me in three years? That didn't mean anything. In fact, Jack was my ticket to Simon's heart and the career of my dreams.

What I needed to do was bury any temptation beneath one of Sage's accidental avalanches, and focus on the task at hand. Which would be easier if I could sleep! I forced my eyes closed and tried counting sheep.

One fluffy lamb…then two…

A blaze of white light seared through my eyelids. The sheep vanished as I pried my eyes open and quickly shielded them against the fluorescent assault. Beams of vivid light poured through the picture window, illuminating the room as if it were daytime.

I rolled out of bed and stumbled to the window, nearly tripping over my half-empty suitcase. My hands searched for a string to lower the blinds, but there wasn't one. To my horror, none of the windows even had curtains. Another laugh, this one delirious, tore from my chest. *Irony meet my best friend insomnia.*

There had to be something I could use to block the light, but a quick search of the room, and its lack of amenities, made me realize it was pointless. I also realized I'd fallen prey to another one of Jack's schemes.

Squinting through the glass, I made out a row of floodlights, all angled toward my room. What usually lit the tree farm so happy customers could pick out their tree past sunset, was now a spotlight of misery, keeping me from slumber. My fists clenched as I searched for Jack beyond the beacons of torment. He was out there, hiding in the shadows, likely celebrating his success.

Short-lived success. He had no idea he was dealing with a witch who valued her sleep. Something I'd had precious little of since checking into the inn. A smug grin sealed his fate as I inhaled a deep breath and channeled a well of magic. Zips of energy flowed down my arm, and with a sharp jab of my finger against the window, the first floodlight winked out. I muttered an incantation and a second jolt of magic extinguished the rest of them, one by one, until only the moon dared to shine its light. And considering its fullness and the lack of curtains in my room, even that celestial body was on my naughty list.

Take that, Jack.

I spun on my heel and threw myself back into bed. In case Jack found any more lights, I pulled the blankets up over my head and buried my face in the pillow. Tomorrow, I'd see about getting some blackout curtains installed. I might even invest in some wildlife repellent and an eye mask. Who knew what other disturbances Jack might send my way? I wouldn't put a visit from a skunk past him.

Just as I was finally drifting off, the deafening sound of a chainsaw split the air. The blade sank into something solid, throttling to an ear-piercing volume. A hiss, not unlike the one from the opossum, slipped through my teeth. Ear plugs were getting added to the shopping list. Shoving my arm through the blankets, I waved it viciously through the air and flared my fingers toward the abrasive sound. The chainsaw sputtered, and for a few blissful seconds, there was silence.

It revved again, and I closed my fist around a ripple of magic, silencing the saw for good. The only sound left was Jack's muffled oath from beneath my window. With his defeat blanketing the farm like newly fallen snow, I fell fast asleep.

***

Day two at the Bradley Inn broke cold and clear, and a thick layer of snow glistened over the farm. After sleeping in as late as I dared, I slipped into the bathroom to take a hot shower and get ready for the day. I was still bemused by my showdown with Jack, and by the strange urge I had to see what he'd try next.

I unpacked my toiletry bag for the second time and grabbed a fresh towel from the rack, then turned on the shower. Humming to myself, I wriggled my fingers under the water, frowning at the icy temperature. The inn was on the older side, but the tub had filled with hot water without issue last night. A sneaky suspicion wrinkled my nose as I spun the hot water dial as far as it would go. Nothing. Just cold water.

The crack of an axe drew my attention, and I tied my robe tighter around my waist and trudged to the window. Jack was in the side-yard, chopping firewood. His shoulder muscles bunched as he drew the axe back, and then forward to let it slice evenly through the log.

Wiping his brow, he chugged water from a bottle, tipping his head back to reveal the strong column of his neck. Honestly, the entire scene would have been guilty pleasure popcorn viewing if I wasn't standing next to a shower raining cold water.

I shoved open the window and leaned my arms against the casing.

"Turn it back on, Jack!" My angry breath came out in white puffs of frozen air. Jack looked up at me with a smirk that said more than enough about my current utility situation.

"Turn what back on? Are you having trouble with something?" He adjusted his work gloves and picked up the axe.

"Yes. There's no hot water."

With a shrug and another muscular swing of the axe that normally would have made my mouth water, he said, "Grandma Jean told you it was tricky. This is an old inn. It happens."

"It worked fine last night. You did something to it, and if you don't fix it right now, I'm going into the basement to fix it myself."

Leaning on the handle of his axe, Jack shook his head. "Unfortunately, all maintenance areas and basement access are closed to guests." He snapped his fingers. "You know who doesn't have trouble with their hot water? The hotel in town."

I growled in frustration. "I'm not leaving, Jack!"

He went back to chopping wood, and I inhaled a shuddering breath of fury. Looking down, I saw a mound of snow gathered within an empty window box. I reached inside and scooped my hand to form a ball, then packed the snow together between my palms. Narrowing my eyes, I blew magic into the snowball, and like a needle penetrating a voodoo doll's limb; I aimed for Jack's back when he bent to reach for another sip of water.

Bullseye!

The snowball hit with perfect precision, and Jack grunted in surprise. I flattened myself against the bathroom wall unable to control a snort of laughter. *Fine. Let him think he's won.* There were other ways to solve my problem. All I had to do was fill the tub and then use a spell to warm the water. The whole process would take longer, but it was a small price to pay.

Pushing away from the wall, I popped the lever on the shower to make the water pour into the tub, only to slump down on the edge when I realized there was no stopper. I searched the bathroom and even went into the room next door where I'd bathed the night before, but the stopper was missing.

"That wretch," I grumbled, marching back to my room. It looked like for the time being it was a cold shower or nothing. Hyping myself up, I dove beneath the icy stream and took the quickest shower of my life, shivering so hard I thought I might knock my head against the tile.

After putting on my warmest clothes and drying my hair, I went downstairs to search for coffee to heat my insides. Grandma Jean stood over the stove stirring a pot of oatmeal.

"Coffee's on the sideboard, dear," she said, setting out a bowl for me and filling it with oatmeal. "Oh, I turned the water heater back on. Jack must have flipped the breaker switch last night, so by this morning the water had cooled. Give it an hour and we'll have hot water again. I hope it wasn't too much of a surprise this morning."

"No, it was fine," I said even though it was pure torture. "I should have expected as much." I polished off my breakfast, watching as Grandma Jean spooned the rest of the oatmeal into an insulated bowl and screwed on the lid. "Is that Jack's breakfast? Mind if I take it out to him? I feel like we've gotten off on the wrong foot and a little one-on-one conversation might help."

"That would be wonderful, dear." She handed me the container and placed the empty pot into the sink.

I bundled up for the weather and tucked the container under my arm, then went to go find Jack. This early, the tree lot was still empty of customers, and Grandma Jean had mentioned business was slow this year. I passed by a cute wreath stand that was fully stocked and then walked past a line of pre-cut trees leaning against a fence.

With a devious flick of my wrist, I sent the trees toppling like dominos. It was petty, but it felt good. Maybe Jack's Scrooge-like tendencies were already rubbing off on me, or maybe turnaround was just fair play.

I found Jack around the corner in the woodshed, stacking the logs he'd chopped. On the ground near the stack was the chainsaw that had interrupted my sleep the night before. He'd taken it apart in an apparent attempt to fix it, but no amount of repairs was going to do the trick. I made sure of that.

Leaning against a post, I unscrewed the bowl's lid

and breathed in the delicious scent of warm oatmeal. Jack paused when he sensed my presence, his whole body tensing.

"Good morning, Jack. Isn't it beautiful out today? The sun is shining, and the wildlife have returned to their nests."

He threw the last log onto the pile and rested his hands warily on his hips.

"Did you enjoy your shower, Delia?"

"It was very invigorating. I've always wanted to do a polar plunge, and now I've had some training."

His eyes locked onto the bowl in my hand. "Is that my breakfast?"

"It is. Did you want some?" I dipped the spoon into the oatmeal and then fluttered it around in the air and took a bite.

Jack's gaze darkened when I went in for a second round. He strolled closer, boots crunching over the hard-packed snow. Right when he was an arm's length away, I tipped the bowl over and let it fall from my hand. Oatmeal spilled to the ground in wet clumps.

"Oops. I dropped it." I pursed my lips into a pout. "Too bad I ate the last of the oatmeal before I came outside. I hope you weren't too hungry."

"I'm starving, Delia. You shouldn't have done that." Careful to avoid his fallen breakfast, he leaned in, lifting a hand to place it above my head on the post, trapping me with his body. My pulse jumped from his closeness and the scent of soap on his skin.

Had he taken a cold shower too?

The air sizzled between us as I watched an array of

emotions filter across his face. Irritation morphing to interest and then settling on something wolfish that made heat pool inside my stomach. I stilled as his thumb brushed the side of my mouth, skimming over my lip.

"You missed some."

Coherent words fled from my mind as his focus remained on my mouth, almost as if he fought himself to taste where his thumb had been.

The harsh ding of a service bell broke the spell and forced us apart. Jack peered around the shed while I blew out a tension-filled breath and tried to put myself back together. That hadn't gone exactly as planned. So much for my cold dish of revenge. Instead, I was thawing at his feet. Thankfully, the bell had rung some sense into my head and reminded me why I was here in the first place.

"I have to deal with a customer," Jack said, turning back to me. I was shocked by the regret that flashed in his eyes, and I backed up a few steps, needing to put some space between us.

"Yeah. I should get back to the inn, myself."

He nodded and left me standing under the woodshed wondering what I'd gotten myself into. None of his pranks had even come close to making me pack my bags. But the look he'd given me while leaning against the post had tested my resolve.

I shook the unsettling feelings away and walked back to the inn, determined to start fresh tomorrow.

CHAPTER 6
Delia

The scent of bacon greeted me when I entered the kitchen the next morning. I stifled a yawn as I slipped into a chair at the counter. Today was the day to put my plan in motion, and it couldn't have come at a better time.

I'd had another sleepless night, tossing and turning, waiting anxiously for one of Jack's pranks, but they never came. I didn't know which was worse, lying in bed waiting in suspense or wondering why they might have stopped.

Grandma Jean wiped her hands on her festive apron and poured me a cup of coffee. With a smile that faltered when she caught sight of my face, she set the cup on the counter and nudged a tray of milk and sugar closer.

"Good gracious, dear. You look exhausted."

I drank deeply from my cup, then waited as Grandma Jean topped it off. "I've been having trouble sleeping. But I'll be fine."

Grandma Jean pressed her lips together and shook her head. "Sorry, dear. I know my grandson has been giving you some trouble. Though you seem to be handling yourself well enough. You made it through the hot water episode, and Jack won't stop grumbling about his broken chainsaw."

"Don't mess with a witch if you value your tools," I said, taking another sip of coffee.

"Well, the good news is your plan is ready for action. Thanks to you, Jack has to go into town to buy a new saw. He should be down any minute. Make sure he gives you a lift." Grandma Jean winked and offered me a plate of scrambled eggs and bacon.

I dug in, savoring the dish and chasing it with the rest of my coffee. Heavy footsteps pounded down the stairs, and I looked up as Jack entered the kitchen. Our gazes clashed, his holding mine while he poured steaming coffee into a tumbler.

"Sleep well, Delia?" Jack leaned leisurely against the counter, dressed in another one of his rugged flannels, and a pair of cargo pants. He refused to look away first. Did he know I tossed and turned all night? By the look of him, he hadn't fared much better. He'd probably stayed up planning his next attack. I shouldn't let my guard down.

I lifted my empty mug in a mock toast. "Like the Princess and the Pea. You are so lucky to live on such a quiet and peaceful, farm. I could stay here forever."

"Oh, that would be lovely, dear," Grandma Jean said with a knowing look.

Jack's stare hardened, and he shoved the cap on his travel mug. "I'm heading into town. I have to stop at the hardware store, and then I'll be back later to open the farm for tree sales."

Grandma Jean cleared her throat, but I was way ahead of her. I planted a wool hat on my head and pushed out of my chair.

"Perfect. You can give me a ride. I have a list from the hardware store too."

"And don't forget my bakery order!" Grandma Jean called after us as Jack barreled out of the house with me on his heels.

Rock salt crunched under my precarious boots, and I lifted a brow as Jack wrenched open the passenger side of his truck.

"I didn't want to get sued. Get in."

I cleared the amusement from my throat and eyed the rundown pickup. It was slightly dented and splattered with mud. The inside wasn't much better, sporting ripped upholstery, and more gravel in the foot well than there was on the driveway. I just hoped the heat worked.

Gritting my teeth, I climbed inside and waited for Jack to start the engine. The radio came on, blasting a version of The Twelve Days of Christmas as we pulled out of the drive and onto the main road. Jack reached for the dial, muttering a curse at every station playing holiday music.

"Why do they insist on playing Christmas carols the entire month long?" he grumbled.

"Oh, come on. It's not that bad. They're classics. There must be at least one holiday song you enjoy."

Jack hit the dial on the dashboard, cutting off the music. "I prefer silence."

Of the Lambs… I rolled my eyes and faced the

window, stuck with the soothing sounds of the rumbling engine. Thick pine trees dusted with snow flew past as we left the rural side of town and turned onto Main Street. Neither of us spoke, but I was too busy taking in the cheerful scene. It was as if we'd left the forest and entered Santa's Village.

Wreaths hung from wrought iron lamp posts, and shop windows were decked out with hanging balls, strings of lights, and paper snowflakes. We passed the town square with a giant gazebo and a platform waiting for the town Christmas tree to arrive. I craned my neck to count the number of skaters on the small rink set up in the square.

Snow flurries blew in the air as Jack parked the truck in front of the hardware store. He steeled himself before getting out of the vehicle, almost as if he was preparing for battle. The creak of the truck door drew every eye in sight, and a flush that could have been the cold, but was more likely insecurity tinted his features.

"Is everything all right?" I asked, as a couple sipping hot drinks bent their heads together and started whispering.

Jack ignored my question and hunkered down in his coat, taking the steps to the shop two at a time. I followed him into the rustic store and wrinkled my nose at the scent of paint and oil that hung thick in the air.

An older man stood behind the counter and he greeted me with a warm smile as I grabbed a basket by the register. Jack didn't receive the same welcome. I watched as the man's smile turned down and his arms crossed rigidly over his chest. *How strange…*

A few of the customers gave Jack a wide berth, some even changing directions to go down another aisle so they wouldn't cross his path. It was hard to watch. Especially the way Jack seemed to ignore the looks, keeping his head high, even though there was the tiniest falter in his step.

Jack's file had notes about the townspeople giving him the cold shoulder. His father had been a pillar in the community and was liked by everyone. The same could not be said for his son. I assumed it was because Jack was Scrooge incarnate, but there had to be more to it.

I filled my basket with a few items, keeping close to Jack as if my presence could somehow lighten the hostility shooting his way. I wasn't sure why I felt so annoyed. Jack had been trying to drive me from the inn, but somehow, my feelings had shifted. That or I was delirious from lack of sleep.

Either way, Jack was my responsibility, and there had to be a way to not only help him find love but also change the attitude of the town. But first things first. I checked the time, surprised to find it was already past nine. We were burning daylight, and I had a match to make.

Jack pulled a new saw off the shelf and hoisted it over his shoulder. I wondered if I'd be neutralizing that one tonight as well. I hoped he had store credit. Our stalemate was going to get expensive.

"Do they make silencers for those things?" I joked, tossing a handful of disposable ear plugs into my basket. "Or maybe I should get one for myself and we can do dueling chainsaws at midnight?"

Jack's mouth hitched as he headed toward the register. "After the last few days, I wouldn't get within twenty feet of you and a blade."

"Hmm...smart man." I placed my basket on the counter and spoke to the older man ringing up our order. "Have you picked out your Christmas tree, sir? You should check out the selection at the Bradley Farm. I hear they're the best in town."

The old man grunted at my sales pitch and gave Jack a dark look. "That farm's still running? I thought it died with your father."

I swallowed against the sour taste in my mouth from the man's retort. But Jack just snatched the receipt and our purchases from the counter and nudged me toward the door. He was silent until we were back out on the street.

"Don't do that," he muttered, locking the saw in the back of his truck.

"I'm sorry." My throat felt tight as I followed him down the shoveled sidewalk. "I didn't realize..."

"No, you didn't realize. But you got a front-row seat, didn't you? Everyone in this town thinks I ruined my father's farm and tainted his legacy. And you know what? They're not wrong." Jack paused in front of a cute little bakery with a hanging wooden sign. He folded his arms over his chest. "I'll wait outside for you to pick up Grandma Jean's order, and then I need to head back to the farm. If you're going to be longer in town, you can get a taxi back or call the farm and I'll send someone to get you."

I peered through the bakery window and spotted a young woman behind the counter. *Becky Santos.* The target of my matchmaking scheme. I couldn't make two people fall in if they weren't in the same room. No. Jack wasn't going anywhere until I'd worked a little magic.

CHAPTER 7
Jack

"Let me buy you a coffee."

Delia's fingers rested on my forearm. Tiny snowflakes latched onto her gloves, making a fine crystal pattern. The flakes caught in her hair too and melted against her cheeks that had turned pink from the cold.

But her fingers lingered. An invitation that I let hang in the air until she rolled her eyes and huffed a frozen breath.

"I know what you're thinking. But I promise not to poison it. I left my case of cyanide back in the room."

"And my saw is in the truck, so I guess that makes the bakery neutral territory."

"Only if you come inside." Delia reached for the door and swung it open, flourishing her hand like an usher inviting me into a show. "Hurry up, you're letting the cold air in," she teased under her breath.

I scraped a hand through my hair and rocked back on my heels with hesitation. The thing was, Delia's offer was tempting—though suspicious—and after yesterday's moment in the woodshed, it was also an offer I should refuse before things got out of control.

Even without the possibility of revenge for what I'd put her through or the temptation of something more, I hadn't spent this much time in public since I'd moved back to Wood Pine. Already the morning was off to a rocky start with the verbal slight at the hardware store. Still, Delia didn't look like she'd take no for an answer, and if I wanted to avoid a scene, coffee was my best bet.

"A quick coffee. Free of toxins," I conceded, passing her to enter the shop. Immediately, the sweet smells of warm pastries and sugar cookies invaded my senses. If you bottled it up, you could label it *Delia Frost*, and sell it in the perfume aisle at Macy's.

The shop was busy, and workers weaved behind the counter making flavored coffees, while wrapping pastries in little cardboard boxes. We stepped into line and Delia nudged me in the shoulder and angled her head toward the woman working the counter.

"Grandma Jean says the pastry chef here makes the best croissants." Delia's voice dipped with a sly murmur. "She also mentioned the young woman might be an old flame. Care to comment?"

I scoffed. "Who Becky? Don't be ridiculous. We were in the same class and chatted a bit, but that was about it. She had plans after graduation to start her own bakery in the city, but they fell through and she took the open bakery position here instead." I mimicked Delia's devious tone. "What's with the interest? Are you jealous?"

Delia threw her head back and laughed. "Dream on, Conifer Casanova. I don't swoon at the feet of men who try to run me out of town."

"Not town, just my inn, and no one's running in those boots."

The line moved as we inched our way to the front.

Delia chewed on her lip, her nose wrinkling in irritation. She was probably calculating the deadly dose of cinnamon. *For when you forget to bring your cyanide.* She was definitely up to something. Her gaze darted around the cafe, taking it all in like she was concocting some sort of scheme. Maybe she planned to rob the place. I still didn't know why she'd come to town. A laugh rumbled in my chest at the thought. Delia, the Candy Cane Bandit.

When we reached the front, Becky—my supposed admirer, did a double take. Most people did when they spotted me, but rarely with a friendly smile. To be fair, Becky was the only one in town who didn't seem to care about my past. But that didn't mean I wanted to date her and drag her down to the depths of my despair.

Plus, she wasn't nearly as fiery as...

"Jack, it's nice to see you. It's been a while." Becky's smile deepened, interrupting my dangerous line of thought. "I have your grandmother's order in the back. But can I get you anything else?"

I shrugged, barely looking at the specialty menu. "Large coffee, black."

Delia cleared her throat and leaned in to mutter, "Come on, live a little. This is my treat. Pick out your favorite pastry and order something you wouldn't normally get. Something with foam and sprinkles of cinnamon."

See, she's planning something nefarious with spices.

"Fine. A cheese danish and a large cappuccino, extra shot of espresso. *No* cinnamon. Then whatever my—" I glanced at Delia, stumbling over what to call her. We weren't friends. Nemesis was closer. I certainly couldn't call her the stranger who'd invaded my home, and my thoughts for the past forty-eight hours.

Delia answered for me. "I'm staying at the inn for a few weeks, and Jack offered without hesitation to give me a ride into town this morning. He's such a great guy."

Was that sarcasm? Yeah, there were distinct bitter undertones in Delia's reply. But the mockery must have gone over Becky's head because she nodded, her auburn curls bouncing.

"He is," she insisted. "I've always thought so." Becky's lashes fluttered, and a foreboding sensation seized my spine. I gauged Delia's reaction, but she was nodding too with a look of innocent approval on her face.

That's it. She's tasting my coffee first.

Delia ordered some fancy latte with extra whipped cream that came in a giant ceramic mug, and we took our orders to a small table along the wall. I listened skeptically as Delia gushed over Becky's sweet personality and supposedly fashionable pastry chef outfit. It was a white coat. How did you make that fashionable?

"She's really cute, and successful! And look—" Delia wriggled her fingers, then pointed at my cappuccino. "Becky made a heart in your foam. I think she likes you."

Okay…things were getting weird. There wasn't anything etched in my foam on the walk to the table. I know because I checked to make sure there wasn't cinnamon dust lurking in my cup. But sure enough, there was a heart now. The foreboding was back, coupled with an odd suspicion. First, the floodlights had gone out on their own, then my brand new saw bit the dust, and I'd spent a good ten minutes picking up the fallen trees by the woodshed that had been fine five minutes earlier. All mysterious events that took place strangely around Delia. Not to mention her uncanny aim from a second-floor window. I might not have witnessed it, but Delia hit me with that snowball.

"Huh, interesting." My lips flattened into a grim line.

"That's it? It's just interesting?" Delia's shoulders slumped, and she sucked a bunch of whipped cream from the top of her cup. "It's more than just interesting. It's a sign."

I lifted my brow. "A sign?"

"Yeah, a signal from the universe. Sometimes guardian angels go out of their way to make things happen." Delia gritted her teeth. "It's vital you pay attention."

A laugh choked the back of my throat. "I think it's just coffee art. It's artisanal. That's why it costs so much."

Delia's nose twitched. I really enjoyed riling her up, and the coffee wasn't half bad either. I sipped from my cup until the heart became just a smudge in the foam. Then I went in for the kill.

"So since you aren't going to be leaving my inn anytime soon, what exactly are you doing here in Wood Pine?"

Delia took her time, savoring more of the whipped

cream. My gaze followed her tongue as she licked some from the top of her lip.

"I'm a writer for an obscure magazine, and I'm doing an article on your grandmother's Spells and Brews Ladies' Club for our holiday edition. You've probably tried her Winter's Moon Spiced cider. I'm including the recipe."

"Ah, you're one of them."

"Excuse me?"

"You know, mystical people."

Delia shoved a lock of hair out of her face and scowled. "Let me guess. You don't believe in magic."

"I grew up with Grandma Jean, so just the opposite. I'm a firm believer. But lately—mostly in the last day or two—I believe in curses."

"Very funny," Delia mocked while I tried to contain another laugh. We drank our coffee in silence for a few moments until she motioned back toward Becky.

"I hope everything's okay over there."

Becky paced in the corner with a cell phone to her ear. Her features were drawn tight, and she whispered urgently into the handset. When she ended the call, she grabbed a bag sitting on the counter and approached our table.

"Here's your grandmother's order." Becky's voice wobbled as she placed the bag next to me.

"Is something wrong?" Delia asked. "That didn't look like a pleasant phone call."

Becky sighed and rubbed the lines between her forehead. "That was my father. He's the mayor and responsible for getting the town's Christmas tree set up in the square. But there's a problem with the distributer this year, and now there's no tree. He's very upset."

"I'm sorry to hear that," Delia said, stepping on my foot.

I glared at her from across the table as her eyes widened with a mischievous look. *Nope. Not happening.* I shook my head. She kicked my shin. Air hissed through my teeth from the sharp pain. That one was going to bruise.

"Jack's farm can provide a tree," Delia offered, ignoring the slicing gesture I made under my chin. The threat only made her bolder. "Why don't you come to the farm tomorrow and help us find the perfect tree? Jack would love to have you."

Becky beamed. "Are you sure? That would be fantastic, but I know that there's been some—"

"Mutual hostility between me and the town," I cut in.

Delia spoke over me. "Which is why it's a great idea! Not only will it help your father out of a jam, but it might help smooth things over with people. Plus, it will be great for business at the farm, and for my article."

"It really would be a lifesaver," Becky said, smoothing her hands down her apron. "Let's do it! I'll be by in the afternoon."

"Perfect." Delia lifted her cup and clinked it into mine while it was still sitting on the table. "It's a date."

Becky flushed, and my frown deepened.

"Fine. Don't get your flannel shirt in a twist." Delia rolled her eyes at me. "It's not a date. It's a meeting of like-minded tree hunters on a quest to save the town's Christmas. How's that?"

"Sounds like I have to pick my poison," I drawled.

Delia sent me a wink. "Then I'd choose wisely."

CHAPTER 8
Delia

Melting Jack's heart would not be easy.

My magical attempt at coffee art had not piqued his interest, and so I'd made a last-ditch effort before we left to materialize a flirty note for Becky on a napkin. I just hoped it would prove useful. But in all honesty, it wasn't some of my best work. Ever since we'd stepped into the bakery, I'd felt off-center. Maybe it was from the combative back and forth with Jack that I somehow enjoyed even though his remarks were grumpy as ever.

Was I attracted to scathing wit? Surely not. Simon never talked like that. He didn't challenge everything you said or poke holes in your argument. He was conventional. Perfect on paper and in person. Kind of like Becky. Which was another thing...

I frowned in front of the mirror letting the curling iron in my hand sit for too long on a single section of hair. Becky was nice. She had a great job, made delicious pastries, and had a smile like a beauty queen. I should be outside making snow angels, she was so flawless.

So why did I want to kick a snowman instead?

The scent of burning hair jolted me back to the mirror. With a curse, I unwound the scorched section and ran my fingers through the loose curls. My confusing feelings and indecision didn't matter. The only thing I knew for certain was that I needed to work harder.

Not even my push to hype Becky's many positive traits had seemed to sway Jack. I didn't expect this case to be easy or solvable on the first try, but I thought I'd at least get a spark of something romantic from Jack's side. He was a living, breathing man, after all. Even just a half smile as she fixed our drinks or a covert glance toward the counter would have given me hope. But I'd gotten nothing!

Jack's heart was colder than the icicles hanging from the roof of the inn. The case file should have listed the cheese danish as the future love of his life. Now that I could work with.

Which was why when a promising opportunity presented itself, I chose to dig deep and expose old wounds. Not only had I scored a second—*not a date*—encounter, but I'd thrust Jack's farm into the spotlight. Donating a tree was a brilliant start to changing his reputation with the people of Wood Pine.

Sure, it wasn't a perfect start, on paper or otherwise, but it was something.

Time to go pick out a Christmas tree, and earn my promotion. After packing away my curling iron, and applying a slick layer of vanilla-scented lip gloss, I wrapped a thick scarf around my neck, stuffed my feet into my boots, and zipped up my coat. Jack was already somewhere outside, likely cursing my name at getting him involved with the town's holiday preparations.

Becky was supposed to meet us soon, and then we'd hike through the farm with me lagging behind working some behind-the-scenes sorcery.

Stepping outside onto the wraparound porch, I blew warm air into my palms to charge up the spells, then slipped on a pair of wool mittens. A few gray clouds hung overhead, giving me the perfect opportunity to cast a brief snow squall.

Strolling through the pine trees while big fluffy flakes fell from the sky seemed like the ideal atmosphere for flirtation. Then when we were finished and Becky had left for the evening, I'd conjure a surprise special delivery containing Jack's favorite cheese danish. *Always leave them wanting more...*

It was a throwback, but if the way to a man's heart was through his stomach, it was a good thing Becky was a pastry chef.

Becky's car pulled down the driveway, and she gave me a cheery wave as she climbed out of the vehicle. She was dressed in an olive green puffy coat and a pair of dark skinny jeans. Her copper-colored hair flowed down her back, and an off-white hat with a fuzzy pom-pom sat on her head. She looked like a heroine returning to her small hometown from the plot of a holiday rom-com, and seeing her caused that odd sensation to tingle the back of my neck again. The one where I wanted to unleash my frustrations on a frozen sculpture.

I forced excitement on my face and returned her wave. "Hey, Becky. Thanks for coming."

"My pleasure! This was such a great idea. It's always been a town tradition to display a Bradley Farm's tree. A few years ago they started using a large-scale distributor, so it'll be nice to restart the tradition."

"Was your father okay with it?"

Becky made a face as I joined her on the gravel path that led to the acreage at the back of the inn. "He knows it's the right thing to do. But I'd be lying if he didn't grumble about it. I wish everyone would put the past in the past. The accident wasn't Jack's fault."

Accident? Grandma Jean had gone into detail on Jack's current situation, but she'd been light on his past. All I had were the few notes in his case file. But there hadn't been anything about an accident. We paused in front of the barn, and since we were still alone, I asked the question weighing on my mind.

"What accident? Was someone hurt?"

Becky kept her voice low. "No. Nothing like that." She paused and looked over her shoulder. "Since you're staying in town for a while, you're going to hear the gossip. You might as well hear it from me. Two years ago, Jack had a falling out with his father over a broken engagement. Honestly, I'm glad the deal fell through. It would have been a marriage of convenience and that wasn't fair to Jack. He deserves more than the deed to the neighboring land. He deserves someone who can give him everything." She blushed at her answer and sheepishly let her gaze roam over the barn. Clearing her throat, she said, "Grandma Jean told me once that Jack refuses to go inside the barn ever since he came back. They did a nice job rebuilding. You can't even tell there was an incident."

"What happened?" I asked, wishing Becky would

stop with the vague accident references and get to the point.

"Well, the reason Jack left was—"

Jack stepped around the side of the barn, a saw slung over his shoulder and his familiar scowl on full display. Becky startled and let out a high-pitched yelp as if she'd stumbled across an angry yeti brandishing a weapon.

I sighed at Jack's untimely entrance. "Don't worry about the saw, Becky. You get used to it."

"It's a tree farm. How else do you expect me to cut the trees?" Jack grumbled. He eyed both of us and attempted a tight smile. "Ready to get this over with?"

"I think what our rugged farm guide means is, the best trees are that way." I pointed down the path and waved my two reluctant love birds forward. Jack met my gaze over Becky's head, and I pressed my lips together to keep from laughing. He looked miserable. But that would change once we got going. I planned to rip his romance-averse Band-Aid right off, and I'd start with a little atmospheric snow.

With the two of them walking ahead, I took off my mittens and rubbed my palms together. Magic tingled in my fingers as more gray clouds gathered and the first few flakes fell. The ground crunched beneath my feet, a mix of packed snow and fallen pine needles as I followed them down the trail and into the rows of trees. At first glance, I could see how the farm had fallen on hard times. Many of the trees were overgrown and needed shearing, and some had gaping bare spots that even the largest ornaments couldn't hide.

But there was also something mesmerizing about

the vast field. As if beauty lay in the wild, untamed landscape. With some care and attention, so much potential and future memories remained. It reminded me of why I wanted to become an agent. *Miracles happen with love and a little magic.*

The crisp air was invigorating, and I breathed it in, feeling recharged from the fresh pine aroma. This was going to work. Already, I felt light-hearted and slightly dreamy as we weaved through the field rich with festive history and family traditions.

"How about this one?" Becky pointed toward a modest pine that was leaning slightly to the left. Its branches were full, so it had that going for it, but it wasn't what I pictured headlining the town square. We needed a showstopper, and I had to believe there was one hidden further in the back.

"Fine by me." Jack hefted the saw off his shoulder.

I held up my hand. Regardless of my opinion on Becky's selection, we couldn't pick a tree in the first ten minutes! Becky and Jack hadn't even chatted. All we'd done was walk in awkward silence listening to the sounds of our footsteps. Only the ambiance was top-notch. The flirting was non-existent.

"Wait. I don't think that's the one. We should keep looking. We'll know it when we see it."

A wistful smile transformed Jack's features, and for an instant, his gaze softened. He lowered the saw to the ground and rested his hands on his hips. "That's what my dad always said to customers. 'You'll know it when you see it.' Like there was a specific tree for each family."

Something warm kindled in my chest as Jack let his

guard down. It might be brief, but it renewed my hope. I wandered a short distance away, pretending to search for another tree, hoping Becky might take advantage of Jack's blink-and-you-might-miss-it vulnerability.

Twirling my finger, I made a rush of snowflakes swirl around her body like a crystal halo. Another spell infused the air with a hint of cinnamon and vanilla—both aphrodisiacs that should increase the chances of evoking desire. Becky's cheeks were flushed from the cold, and she looked like a snow queen standing among her evergreen subjects.

But she didn't take the hint.

Geez, Becky. I'm literally doing all the work here. At least give him a charming anecdote from your family to share in the moment.

"Um..." Becky broke the silence, and I perked up, certain she was about to reveal a gem. "What kind of tree is this one?"

"It's a Fraser fir."

"Ah, yes. That's a good one. Excellent needle retention."

I dropped my head into my hands and rubbed my temples. Their conversation was headache-inducing. *Less words, more physical contact.*

Pushing my palms forward, I sent a gust of wind into Becky's back. She stumbled into Jack with a nervous yelp, and he caught her around the shoulders, keeping her on her feet. Her head tilted back, and their eyes met. The air settled, and it was like I was watching time stand still as the tension thickened.

I could barely breathe, and my chest hurt. Pricks

of tears stung the corners of my eyes as the urge to separate them with another blast of icy air moved through me, tempting my fingers until I closed my hands into fists. This was what I wanted! I chanted another name in my head, hoping it would dim the buzzing.

Simon…Simon…Simon—

Jack released Becky and gave her a friendly pat on the shoulder. "Watch your step. It's icy out here."

Relief poured through me, and I ducked behind one of the trees to squeeze my eyes shut. What was wrong with me? I needed to get my head on straight or I'd be stuck as an underappreciated office drone for the rest of my life. Closing my hands around a tree branch, I let the prickly needles bite my palm. The sting was soothing in the face of my jealousy. And that's what it was, and I hated it.

It was going to ruin everything!

"Are you okay? Or do you want to be alone with the tree?"

Jack's voice punctured my thoughts, and my eyes popped open. Heat scorched the back of my neck. Releasing the branch, I wobbled on unsteady feet, knocking his shoulder as I brushed past him.

"Uh, yeah. I'm fine. I was just testing the tree's firmness." The heat must have moved from my neck to boil my brain. I sounded just like Becky.

Jack laughed, falling into step beside me. "The two of you are very particular in your tree qualifications."

"Well, it's important," I mumbled, feeling the warmth from Jack's body as he blocked the wind.

"The perfect tree won't change anyone's mind," Jack said under his breath.

I swallowed around the lump in my throat and scanned the rows of trees. The snow kept falling, fluttering gently around our feet. Becky hiked a few rows parallel to us, but I still felt like Jack and I were in a world of our own.

"I couldn't help but notice there seems to be a bit of tension between you and the villagers," I said with a cautious tone.

"Was it because they were all carrying pitchforks? I'm surprised you didn't grab one and march with them."

"I don't hate you, Jack."

His steps slowed. "You don't?"

I shrugged and side-stepped some overgrown branches. "It's amazing how you can see things differently when you're not being chased out of your accommodations."

"Yeah, well, I needed a break. Being a small-town villain is exhausting."

Walking backward, I skimmed my fingers over a pine branch and wiggled my eyebrows. "I wouldn't know. I only spread cheer and joy wherever I go."

Jack's gaze glinted with humor. "You're pure evil dressed up in tinsel and you know it."

"Tinsel is for amateurs. I prefer long garlands of popcorn and cranberries. It's vintage. Like my boots."

My cheeks ached from trying to suppress a grin, and I had to pull myself back together. Flirting with Jack while strolling the tree farm was not part of my plan!

Where was Becky? I searched between the trees for her, and that's when I saw it.

There it is...

The tree stood like a beacon among its neighbors. It was beautifully shaped with even branches, reaching at least eighteen feet tall. A bloody miracle considering most of the trees we'd seen were mediocre at best and much shorter. But this was what we were searching for. Anticipation thrummed through my veins as I imagined it strung with colorful lights in the center of town.

"Over there!" I shouted, gesturing for Jack to follow me as I took off running toward the tree.

"Delia, wait! The grounds uneven, don't—"

Jack's warning reached me at the same time the heel of my boot plunged into a shallow hole. Off balance, I tried to catch myself, planting my other foot on the ground, but the surface was crusted with ice, and I slipped. Not even magic could save me as I fell forward, sprawling face-first into a mound of fluffy snow.

CHAPTER 9
Jack

Delia lifted her face from the snow and pulled pine needles out of her mouth. I knew those boots were trouble, and under any other circumstance, I would have said, 'I told you so', but the wisecrack flew from my mind when Delia winced and grabbed her ankle. I kneeled by her side, worry twisting knots inside my stomach.

"Are you okay? Does it hurt anywhere else?" I asked, startled by the rasp in my voice and the tremble in my hands as I checked her calves for broken bones.

"No. It's just my ankle. I think I twisted it when I fell. But it's fine. See?" Delia tried to rotate her foot and ended up sucking in a pained breath.

It was not fine. She'd likely sprained her ankle. I brushed snow off the side of her face and turned her chin up so she met my gaze. "What were you thinking? There are roots and rocks, and areas that are sheer ice out here."

"I found the perfect tree," she said as if that made up for her injury. Looking over her shoulder, she pointed at the towering pine a few feet away.

My eyes widened when I spotted it. *That tree grew*

on my farm? It was a classic. The kind you see in glossy home and garden magazines. I blinked, thinking it would shift back to a mangy, unkempt fir like all the others. But it didn't. It remained jaw-dropping.

"See, I told you so." Delia nudged my shoulder, her smile as dazzling as the tree in front of us. And for a moment, I had the baffling thought that this amazing tree grew especially for the woman dusted in snow and pine needles at my feet.

"That was my line," I said, returning my focus to her injury. "Let's get you back to the inn and put some ice on that ankle."

Becky stepped into view, and her features contorted in concern when she saw Delia on the ground.

"Oh no. What happened? Can you walk?" She crouched next to us, resting a gloved hand on Delia's shoulder.

"I'm sure I can walk. But we can't leave without our tree."

"Not a chance. With a tree that size, I'll need help with cutting and transporting. Besides, it's not going anywhere. We'll tag it, and I'll come back for it after I round up some extra hands." I passed Becky a length of bright red ribbon and asked her to tie it around a branch. While Becky marveled over the tree, I helped Delia stand. Her leg was bent in the air like a flamingo as I steadied her.

"You sure you can put weight on it?"

Delia wrinkled her nose in annoyance. "I think I know my own foot."

She lowered her boot to the ground and took a

confident step. Her ankle buckled beneath her, and she lurched sideways before I caught her around the waist.

"Wow. Impressive. You should take that act on the road. Oh, wait..."

"Jack," Delia said from between gritted teeth. "It pains me more than a sprained ankle to ask, but can you please help me?"

"I thought you'd never ask." I scooped her off the ground with my arm under her knees. Her head almost cracked my chin when she looked up at me with a little growl.

"That's not what I meant. Ever hear of letting me use you as a crutch?"

"This is quicker," I murmured close to her ear. *And far more enjoyable.*

With an adorable grunt, she settled in my grip and wrapped an arm around my neck. A foreign feeling loosened something inside my chest, and I tightened my hold. I wasn't sure how I'd gone from revving a chainsaw outside her window in the middle of the night to holding her in my arms, but I wasn't disappointed in the trajectory.

Snow continued to fall as the three of us trekked back to the inn. Becky carried my saw, and I carried Delia. And for the first time since I'd met her, Delia had gone quiet. No sarcastic remarks. No witty barbs. Just a contented silence while she rested her head against my shoulder.

After placing Delia on the sofa in the common area, I promised Becky I'd have the tree delivered to the town square before the holiday festival and then sent her on her way so I could tend to Delia's ankle. Grandma Jean found me in the kitchen searching the freezer for an ice pack.

"You didn't trip her, did you?" she whispered, reaching past me to grab a bag of frozen peas. "Here use this. And get the first aid kit under the sink."

"Grandma Jean! No, I didn't trip her."

"Just checking. You two have been at each other's throats. The poor thing. I'm going to put on some hot water and check my recipes for a tea that will help ease her pain. Oh!" She snapped her fingers and asked, "Did you find a tree?"

"Oddly enough, we did. I don't know if it will fix anything, but it's a good tree, grandma. I didn't think there were any left out there."

Grandma Jean squeezed my shoulder. "Must be magic, dear. Now go help our guest. I'll keep an eye out for any customers, but I doubt there will be any. The snow is really coming down out there. I hope we don't get snowed in."

Snowed in? Why did I suddenly wish it would snow harder? Impassable roads meant I wouldn't have to deal with any tree seekers, and Delia couldn't leave, and—*wait.* I shook my head to clear the dangerous thought. I might not be deliberately trying to relocate her anymore, but that didn't mean I wanted to shack up in ugly sweaters and drink eggnog. Did it?

I hated Christmas. Carolers actively avoided spreading holiday cheer within a hundred-foot radius around my inn. Santa probably has a no-fly zone over my farm. There was no way Delia, a woman with holiday spirit coming out of her ears was going to end up with someone like me.

So let it snow until the white stuff reached the roof. She'd probably just strap her pesky poinsettia to her back and snowshoe out of here.

I ground my molars and grabbed the first aid kit, then went to find Delia. While I was gone, she'd taken off her boots and had propped her injured ankle up on a sofa pillow. Somehow, she'd also managed to light the fire in the hearth, and the room was bathed in a cozy orange glow. I looked around for matches but didn't find any. This woman was suspiciously resourceful.

Digging through the first aid kit, I found an elastic bandage and removed it from the pack.

"You've been awfully quiet since we left," I said, crouching in front of her to gently place the bag of peas over her ankle.

Delia grimaced in pain and fiddled with the mittens in her lap. "I just can't believe what a disaster today has been. It was a total failure."

"A failure? That's not how I see it. Thanks to you, Bradley Farms is donating an incredible tree to the town. If it had been left to Becky and I, we would have settled for that first one with the awful lean."

Delia let out a delicate snort and covered her nose with her fingers. "The two of you are a pair. I thought for sure we were going to throw darts and cut the first tree they hit."

I grinned and adjusted the makeshift ice pack. "I'm terrible at darts. We'd still be out there."

"And I probably wouldn't have sprained my ankle."

"After today, we're retiring those boots. I'll find you a pair of Grandma Jean's. You're the same size." I reached for the elastic bandage, and then carefully removed her sock. With painstaking hands, I wrapped the bandage around her ankle. She watched my every movement, barely making a sound until I was finished.

"You're good at that."

"My dad taught me. You're not the first person to fall on the farm. Grandma Jean might be the medicinal guru with her many potions, but I'm the one to come to for cuts and scrapes. You'll have to take it easy for a couple of days, but it's only a light sprain so you should be up and moving by the festival. The Spells and Brews Ladies' Club always set up a booth. You won't want to miss it."

Delia blinked in confusion, then nodded. "That's right, my article. I'm on a deadline." She paused, then gave me a sheepish look. "Thank you for carrying me back. You were surprisingly helpful for a villain."

"Or maybe I'm just misunderstood."

"Maybe."

Her gaze met mine, and I held it, unable to look away. There was a softness in her expression that I'd never seen from her before. My hand still rested lightly on her ankle, and she shifted to the edge of the sofa, the mittens falling from her lap to the floor. The heat from the fire, and the crackle in the air wrapped around us, drawing us even closer together.

Without thinking, I lifted my hand to brush the side of her cheek, letting my fingers linger at the back of her neck. The softness of her skin and her sharp inhale made my heart thud loudly in my ears. Awareness thrummed through my veins as her lips parted and tension thickened the air.

Inches apart, I could feel her breath, warm and mingling with my own. The scent of vanilla and sugar infused my senses, and I knew I'd taste them on her lips. Hoped to. Her eyes softly closed, and the whisper of my name on her next breath was all I needed to hear.

A loud thud broke the silence, and Delia jerked back before our lips met. Her eyes opened wide. A curse caught in the back of my throat as the door opened, and the overhead lights flicked on. Grandma Jean stood in the doorway, ushering a man rolling a wheeled suitcase into the room.

"It's right this way. Your room is on the second floor. Take a right at the top of the stairs."

Another guest? In this weather? I groaned inwardly, wishing I'd had the forethought to take down the vacancy sign. So much for the impassable roads. Was a snowslide too much to ask for?

Delia turned to face the newcomer and nearly forgot she had a sprained ankle. Her features twisted in shock, jaw opening as she stuttered a few incomprehensible syllables.

"S-Simon? What are you doing here?"

Simon? The name was like a lead pipe to the back of the head. This couldn't be the Simon whose name graced her infernal poinsettia? Also known as, Delia's Greatest Gift Ever! My luck was bad, but not that bad.

"Do you two know each other?" Grandma Jean asked, confusion knitting her brow.

"Uh, yes!" Delia hopped around the edge of the sofa

to stand next to Simon. My fists clenched as she latched onto his arm to keep her balance. "This is my…um…my photographer!"

She brushed snow from his jacket sleeve and then gestured toward the stairs. "Simon, you should have been here hours ago. It's already getting late. You should get settled into your room. Mine is right next door. We have a lot of…shots to go over. A whole storyboard."

Of course, they'd be sharing a wall. How wonderful. My insides iced over at the thought of Delia slipping into his room to meet her deadline. Working late by an intimate fire. Sharing coffee first thing in the morning.

Ugh. Where was my saw when I needed it?

"There's no way you're going up and down stairs on that foot. You're changing rooms again," I grated.

Delia's mouth flattened into an exasperated line. But Grandma Jean came to my aid.

"No, Jack's right. We'll move you into a room on the first floor."

Simon's gaze bounced between the three of us. "Right. Then I will meet you in the morning to discuss everything. Sorry to disturb your evening." He turned to leave but paused. "Oh, by the way, this was sitting on your front porch. I think whatever is inside might be frozen."

Simon lifted a small cardboard box tied with a gold ribbon from the top of his suitcase. He handed it to me, then retreated from the room, heading for the staircase.

Delia squeezed her fist against her mouth and cringed. "Oops, the danish."

"How do you know what it is?" I asked, opening the

lid. Sure enough, it was a cheese danish with a little card tucked beside it with a note from Becky.

Because it's your favorite. xoxo Becky.

"Um, she mentioned she was going to leave it for you. It was supposed to be a surprise," Delia said, scratching the back of her neck.

Grandma Jean nodded and glanced covertly at Delia. "Becky's thoughtful like that. Come with me, dear. I'll gather your stuff and bring it downstairs."

I watched Delia shuffle from the room with Grandma Jean's assistance, then I sank onto the sofa. With an agitated growl, I tossed the frozen danish onto the coffee table. *Talk about a disaster.* The bag of peas had thawed, and the fire had slowly dwindled to nothing but a few weak flames. Without its warm glow, the room was as unwelcoming as the barren Christmas tree perched in the corner. I dropped my head into my hands, doing my best to not relive my last few moments with Delia before Simon's unwanted arrival. But it was impossible.

Three was definitely a crowd, and unless Simon kept his distance, it was going to be a long two weeks until Christmas.

CHAPTER 10
Delia

Sprained ankles were the worst. You couldn't even pace properly. With a frustrated groan, I collapsed onto the cushioned window seat and leaned my forehead against the cold glass. Six inches of fresh powder covered the ground. Evidence that you shouldn't cast a magical snowstorm, and then forget to cancel it. And you definitely shouldn't forget that you left an enchanted pastry sitting on the front porch, freezing in the elements.

But in my defense, I'd been a little distracted. And by distracted, I meant holy holly berries, I'd almost kissed Jack.

I blamed the cozy fire—that I'd magically lit for warmth, not atmosphere, though it kind of backfired—and the way Jack smelled like fresh pine during a manufactured snow squall. He'd literally carried me across a frozen tundra and then bandaged my ankle. *A girl can only take so much.*

But then Simon showed up and poured a gallon of icy water on the fire. And by fire, I meant the hots I had for Jack. *Ugh! No. No. No.* This couldn't be happening. Why was Simon here, anyway? It made no sense. Agents didn't work in pairs, and there were a million other small towns at Christmastime to perform miracles. The agency wouldn't send us to the same place.

Unless... Maybe this wasn't the agency at all, but the universe trying to knock some sense into my romance-starved brain. I'd been pining after Simon for three years, and right when I was close to attracting his attention, and getting everything I'd ever wanted, I was sabotaging myself. This was just destiny swooping in to keep me on track.

I glanced at my poinsettia sitting on the nightstand and frowned as a leaf came loose and fell softly to the floor. A few other leaves had already met their demise sometime overnight. *That can't be good.* Had I forgotten to water it?

A soft knock on my door made me jump, and I limped from the window seat to open it and poked my head into the hall. Simon greeted me with a cool smile and a mug of steaming coffee in each hand. He was dressed in a pressed suit with a holiday tie expertly knotted around his neck. A little formal for the Bradley Inn, but not for Simon. *I wonder what he'd look like in flannel?*

"I brought reinforcements," Simon said, handing off one of the mugs. His mouth twisted in distaste as he surveyed my messy appearance and bandaged ankle. "You look like you could use it."

"Yeah, well, it's been a week," I said, peering in both directions and listening for any other signs of movement. When I was sure the coast was clear, I waved Simon inside my room. "Quick, before anyone sees you."

"Why are photographers not allowed in the first-floor bedrooms?" he asked dryly.

"It's part of my cover story." I closed the door behind him and leaned against the wood, taking a life-saving sip of caffeine. "As far as anyone's concerned, I work for an occult magazine, and I'm featuring Grandma Jean's Spells and Brews Ladies' Club in our holiday edition."

Simon nodded and rested a shoulder against the bedpost. Everything felt surreal. The man of my dreams was currently sipping coffee in my bedroom, and instead of feeling joy, I was trying to stave off a stress-induced headache.

He shrugged. "It's not a bad ruse. But what are you going to do when they want to order a copy?"

I nearly choked on my coffee. I hadn't thought about that. "Photoshop, and a little bit of magic?"

"That could work, and actually your story fits well for my purposes." He tipped his mug in my direction. "Good work, Frost."

"What are you doing here?" I asked. My eyes narrowed with suspicion. "Is this about my trial period? I'm doing great. Right on schedule for a miracle. You can let the agency know there's no need for check-ins."

Simon shook his head and drained his coffee. "It's true the agency is often nervous about first-timers, but this isn't about that. I'm here to work a case." He pulled his phone from his suit pocket and scrolled until he found what he was looking for. Turning the device, he displayed a close-up photo of a smiling young woman wearing a white chef's coat.

"Wait. You're here for Becky Santos? There must be a mixup. She's part of my case."

Simon frowned and checked his phone. "There's no mistake. Becky Santos is my target. The case file says it's always been her dream to win one of those prime-time holiday baking competitions and open up a fancy pastry shop in the city. So I'm here to make that happen, and it's a tight deadline. It just came across my desk. Usually, I have more lead time. I've had to pull quite a few magical strings back home to make things happen."

I pinched the bridge of my nose and hobbled back to the window seat. This was a disaster! Becky couldn't leave town now. It would ruin my plan and effectively my case. Not that I wanted to stand in the way of anyone's dreams, but I couldn't start over. How was I supposed to make Jack fall in love at Christmastime with a complete stranger? I might be a miracle worker, but I wasn't bold enough to think I could pull off a love-at-first-sight match on my first try. Those were saved for level three agents at least!

Besides, case files were never wrong. The information was rock solid, based on a mystical formula that was way above my pay grade. If I couldn't make it work, that was my failure, not the agency's.

What was I going to do? Disappointment stabbed me behind the ribcage.

"I'm going to lose the promotion, aren't I?" *And the cute office right next to Simon. And his respect. Plus, I'm going to be stuck doing Agatha's menial tasks forever.* Seriously, at this point, I was a candidate for a miracle. Why weren't they sending someone out for me?

Simon cocked his head and gave me a quizzical look. "It's far more dire than that, I'm afraid."

"What do you mean?"

"The agency guarantee isn't just a saying, it's contractual. There are consequences if we don't complete our missions or if we break the rules. Frankly, I'm surprised you were allowed to work a matchmaking case before you were a full agent. They look easy on paper, but matters of the heart are complicated, and the punishment is severe if you fail."

Unease tickled the back of my neck. "What kind of punishment?"

Simon sighed. "Didn't you read the handbook?"

"I skimmed it," I said defensively. "The thing is over three hundred pages long, and it's all technical jargon. Not that it makes any difference. I don't have time for that now."

Simon smoothed a hand down the front of his tie and picked a piece of phantom lint from his sleeve. Why wasn't he coming up with ideas? Wasn't he going to help me? I knew for a fact he'd solved matchmaking cases before. He always bragged about them at the office. There had to be a solution.

I twisted my hands together as an idea formed. "What if we could still do both cases? There are two weeks left. Give me a few days. A week, tops. The rules don't say Jack can't follow Becky to the city. I mean that's like a huge grand gesture in romantic movies. I would literally swoon if someone did that for me."

"What about the farm? Don't you have to save it or something?"

My headache was back in full force, and my ankle had started to throb. "I don't have all the answers yet. I just need more time. Please, Simon. This promotion means everything to me." *And my romantic future according to Madame Destiny depends on it.*

"All right," Simon hedged. "We can see where you take this. But be careful or you're going to end up on the wrong side of a miracle. I've seen it happen, and it's dark."

"Thank you." I slumped in relief. I wasn't out of the woods, but at least I still had a fighting chance.

"I guess I'd better go into town and buy a camera. You know, accounting hates surprise expenses." Simon collected his empty coffee cup and walked to the door. I exhaled a deep breath as he left and stared out the picture window. In the distance, I spotted Jack, carrying his trusty saw while he headed for the rows of trees alongside a few hired hands. The crew's boots sank deep into the fresh snow, but they plowed forward, on their way to cut our tree.

A soft smile formed on my lips when I remembered the look on Jack's face after I pointed it out. Complete awe. The mark of someone who hadn't thought a miracle was possible. It was heartwarming, and all the proof I needed that Jack deserved to heal and find love.

With Becky. I silenced the invisible elf on my shoulder who snickered and pointed out the obvious: I'd come closer to kissing Jack than she had, and the memory of our almost kiss was hotter than three years of interactions with Simon. But what did invisible elves know, anyway? They weren't bound by a contract or counting on a promotion.

I shook my shoulders loose and shuffled away from the window. What I needed was more coffee and a viable plan. With Jack out in the field, I slipped into the kitchen to refill my mug.

"How's that ankle treating you this morning, dear? Did you enjoy the medicinal tea?" Grandma Jean bustled in from outside, shoving the side door closed behind her. She scraped her boots of snow and tossed her gloves onto the counter.

I reached for an extra mug and poured two cups of coffee. "It's a little sore, but already feeling better. And your tea was delicious. It really helped."

Grandma Jean sipped her coffee and gave me a sly smile over the rim. "Your photographer is handsome. I had a lovely chat with him this morning about camera lenses. Funny how he knew so little."

I ducked my head and pulled my messy hair in front of my face. "I think we both know he's not my photographer. I work with Simon at the agency."

Grandma Jean clucked her tongue. "From that blush, you're trying to hide, it seems you wish you did more than work with him."

"It's complicated. Simon is a top agent and everyone loves him. He has more than his share of admirers. I just wish he'd notice me a little bit."

"Oh, he's not the one for you, dear. He's too stuffy and I'm not getting the right energy. There's no fire there, so to speak."

"But that could change if we were together. I have it on very good authority that it's meant to be."

Grandma Jean's mug clunked to the table. "I hope you're joking. One of my talents is reading people's energies. I can tell instantly when two people are perfect for each other. We've even done readings in our club and put together matchmaking events with great success."

I chewed on the corner of my lip. "Maybe we need something like that for Jack and Becky? We could stage something at the festival to show them they're a good match."

"Dear, I know you're the professional, but I don't think Becky is—"

"When's the next meeting for your ladies' club?" I cut in, excited about the possibilities.

Grandma Jean sighed. "Monday evening. It's my turn to host. We're going to burn a Yule log and drink some of Susan's famous enchanted eggnog."

"That's perfect. I'd love to pitch my idea if that's all right."

"It's fine, dear. Jack usually steers clear of our meetings, so he won't be around."

"Excellent." I grabbed my coffee and hurried back to my room. The festival was only a few days away, and I had plans to make.

CHAPTER 11
Delia

"Who's ready for eggnog? I found the rum!" A woman wearing a festive turtleneck with long silver hair, and dark-framed glasses waltzed into the common room waving a glass bottle.

Grandma Jean leaned over and whispered, "The only thing enchanted about Susan's eggnog is her heavy hand with the rum. Sip slowly, dear."

I smothered a grin, grabbed a cinnamon stick from the bowl on the table, and held up my empty glass. All five ladies gathered inside the common room followed suit, and the December meeting of the Spells and Brews Ladies' Club came to order with the sound of clinking glasses.

Holiday music played from a wireless speaker, and Grandma Jean had prepared savory snacks and trays of cookies, displayed on a red and green tablecloth. A Yule log crackled in the hearth, spitting colorful flames thanks to a few chemical enhancements.

I'd already laid out my plan to the ladies when they'd first arrived, enlisting their help in a matchmaking scheme. All culminating in a strategically placed, mistletoe kiss at their booth. It would be the feature of my "article", and Simon would be there to capture the perfect group photo.

Throw in a little extra magic from my end, and I was counting on this event to be the catalyst that finally brings Jack and Becky together. With the donated tree, and Jack dating the mayor's daughter, he'd be well on his way to healing his rift with the town. After I tied up a few loose ends, I could sit back and let Simon take over. Becky and Jack would be toasting champagne in the city on New Year's Day.

Then he'll be in the same zip code. You might run into them holding hands on the street. The invisible elf was back, whispering destruction in my ear.

I gulped down some more eggnog, wincing from all the enchantment. Grandma Jean watched me from her seat on the couch. She was the only one not giddy with the idea for the festival booth. But she'd come around once she saw the plan in action.

"So, Delia. Truth or Dare, except you can only pick truth. What do you think about our resident Scrooge?" Susan asked, giggling as she ladled another round of drinks into our cups.

I grinned and munched on a cookie, thinking about my answer. "Well, frankly, I'm surprised this place isn't haunted by three ghosts. It's too bad. You could run tours to bring in new guests."

The ladies laughed, raising their cups.

"Maybe we could try to summon some at our next meeting!" Judy, a younger member with a purple streak in her hair and a matching manicure, said. She wriggled her glossy nails. "I'd be happy to lead the seance."

"I'll put it on the planner," Grandma Jean replied with a small tremble in her voice. "Though someone else will need to host. I'm afraid this will be our last meeting at the inn."

"What? No!" All the women chimed in.

"It's true. Jack and I have agreed to sell at the end of the month. You all know he's struggled since he came back, and I love my grandson. I won't force him to be miserable if this isn't what he wants. We'll both use some of the proceeds from the sale to start over. I'm sure there's a charming one-bedroom apartment in town that will suit my needs."

"But the farm has been in your family for generations," Susan said.

"Yeah, there's still hope, Jean. Hold out for a Christmas miracle."

Grandma Jean met my gaze. "Things will happen exactly as they are meant to be. I have faith in that."

My throat tightened with emotion. Grandma Jean was counting on me. I couldn't let her down. But I also couldn't promise her Jack would keep the farm. Now that Simon was here with his new case, everything was up in the air. Though, maybe a fresh start had always been the intention. Sometimes you have to let go of the past to make way for the future.

Reaching across the sofa, I squeezed her hand. In the short time I'd been in Wood Pine, I'd realized how much I enjoyed the small-town feel, and the sense of family, even a fractured one because I could tell beneath it all, there was happiness here, and love. It was something missing in my life, even as I'd tried to chase my own dreams and find someone to share them with.

In our line of work, we were constantly seeing the effects of miracles, and I'd be lying if I said I didn't want to experience a little of that magic for myself. Looking around the room, I could see myself in this club, hosting my own witchy meeting surrounded by delicious snacks and good friends. The scariest truth of all was the possibility I was settling for things that looked good on paper, but in reality, were just as thin.

Behind us, the door creaked open, and I heard Jack's deep voice over the sound of holiday music.

"Ladies, how come my ears are burning?"

Susan laughed and reached for an empty cup. She poured him some of her eggnog, then swayed to the music in his direction. "Darling, we were just enjoying a cocktail while discussing all of your most charming qualities. Please, join us."

"Liars, all of you. Especially you." Jack accepted the glass and pointed the cinnamon stick in my direction.

I shrugged and sipped my cocktail. Grandma Jean rose from the sofa and swirled her finger in the air as if she were rounding up a herd of cats. The ladies all looked at each other with shrewd glances. Judy yawned and reached for her purse. Susan downed her eggnog and swayed into the kitchen. The rest of the group followed, leaving the half-filled punch bowl, and what was left of the snacks.

"So much for my charming qualities." Jack looked over his shoulder, but the group was gone, their voices fading.

"Seriously, I've never seen a room clear that fast."

"You're still here, though."

"Bum ankle. I can't move as fast."

"Ah, that makes sense. Maybe these will help." Jack stepped into the room and hovered near the edge of the sofa. His hand was behind his back, hiding something. "I couldn't find a pair of Grandma Jean's that would work. So I went out tonight and found these. They're yours if they fit. And if not, I still have the receipt."

With a hesitant move, Jack revealed a pair of thick winter boots. They looked cozy and well-insulated with rubber soles to keep out the snow.

My heart swelled, and I couldn't hide my cheesy grin as I reached for them, letting my fingers slide over the soft fur inside. My voice wavered. "I bet these get great traction."

"Yeah, for those spots where people don't put down enough rock salt. It's a real nuisance around here. Someone should say something."

I choked on a laugh as I tried them on, slipping my foot into the soft lining. They were perfect. Easily the nicest pair I'd ever owned.

"Thank you, Jack. I love them."

It was his turn to shrug, but I could tell he was pleased. I tapped the seat next to me and waited for him to sit down. A nervous flutter danced in my stomach. The last time we were in the living room together we'd almost kissed. I was playing a risky game. But I wasn't ready for the night to end. If possible, I wanted it to go on forever, or maybe I could wake up tomorrow and have it start all over like one of those Groundhog Day time loops.

Just for a little while, I promised myself.

Taking a deep sip from my eggnog, I hoped some of Susan's liquid courage would help calm my nerves. Jack was sitting so close, I could feel the heat from his body. His knee brushed mine, and in a bid to distract ourselves, we both leaned forward to take the last sugar cookie.

"You can have it," he said, lifting his fingers from mine. But it was too late, my skin was already tingling from his touch.

I swallowed hard and shook my head, breaking the heart-shaped cookie with red icing and white sugar sprinkles in half. Maybe the rum was going to my head or maybe it was too much sugar, but the way Jack looked at me when I handed him the broken heart made my pulse jump.

Leaning back against the cushion, I cleared my throat and tried to break the friction simmering in the air.

"Wow, you must hate this, holiday songs by a warm fire while sharing the last Christmas cookie. What a nightmare."

Jack's voice was rough around the edges. "Yeah, it's horrible. I may never recover."

The fire snapped and popped, giving off waves of delicious heat.

"Where's your photographer, this evening?" Jack asked, breaking the silence.

"His name is Simon."

"Oh yeah. The man named after a shrub or was it the other way around? I'm not sure."

Was that mild irritation in his tone? Jack drained his eggnog and frowned. Why was I finding his reaction to Simon so endearing?

"I think he went into town for drinks. Simon's not the type to settle in for the evening. He's used to city life. Bars that never close and parties that go till morning."

"And what do you prefer?"

"Definitely this. A low-key evening with good friends."

"What about family? I don't think I've heard you mention anything about them. How come you're working over Christmas and not spending time with them?"

I brushed crumbs from my fingers, and then traced the lines on my palm, reluctant to answer. "I don't have any family. I grew up in foster homes and moved around a lot."

"I'm sorry. I didn't know."

"It's okay. It's not something I like to talk about, but it is a part of me. I think it's one of the reasons I like Christmas so much. That sounds weird to say because I never actually had a real Christmas like other children do. But it was the only time I felt like I could soak up some of the joy around me. Like it lived in the air. As I got older, it was something I looked forward to, and it became this thing where other people experiencing the magic of Christmas allowed me to experience it too. It's why I took the job at—" My mouth snapped closed, and I cursed myself for almost giving away my employer's name. "The magazine. They are very festive."

Jack's gaze had darkened, and he shifted closer, his

arm on the back of the sofa, nearly grazing my shoulder.

"Then you came here, and I tried to get you to leave and grouched at you at every turn. This must be your worst Christmas ever."

"Is it yours?" I murmured.

Jack's fingers skimmed the tips of my hair, and the air lodged in my throat.

"I thought it would be. It should have been. After my dad died last year, and I returned home, I was so mad at everything. It was like I was trapped in a dark hole of grief and anger, and all around me, everyone was preparing for the holidays. It didn't make any sense."

"I'm sorry about your dad. Losing someone is hard, especially at this time of the year." My hand rested against Jack's knee as if my touch could somehow ease the pain in his voice.

"The last time I saw him, we fought, and in those final months that was all we did. He was desperate to expand the farm, and the neighbors wouldn't sell. They wanted the land to stay in their family and the only way we could get access was if I married into it."

Jack scoffed. "It was archaic, and I felt like I was being used to further my father's dream. I went along with it at first, but when the whole thing fell through, I was relieved. But my father was furious. People talked, saying that I was trying to destroy my father's legacy."

"Jack, I'm so sorry. That's awful."

"Don't be. I deserved it. On Christmas Eve, the night before I left, I was so mad after one of our fights that I slept in the barn. I'd been drinking and foolishly left one of the lanterns burning. Somehow it got knocked over and the whole place went up in flames."

"Jack…"

"The worst part was that year, the farm was running a toy drive for a local kids' charity. All the donations were being stored in the barn. Everything was wrapped and ready to be delivered on Christmas morning. But they were lost in the fire. A rumor started that I did it on purpose, so I left town."

"That's ridiculous! You would never—"

"It doesn't matter, Delia. I ruined Christmas for others, kids without families of their own, just like you once experienced. I let this farm die out of anger. There is no joy to soak up here. But the worst part is for the first time in forever, I thought there might be."

Jack's face contorted with anguish as he set his glass down on the table. He pushed off the sofa and stalked to the speaker, silencing it with a jab of the power button. The holiday music cut out, leaving just the sound of the dwindling fire.

"Jack, please don't go, it's not—" I couldn't stop him as he stalked from the room, grabbed his coat off a hook in the hall, and then slammed the front door.

My hands shook as I pressed my fingers against my temple. Learning the truth hadn't changed how I felt. But it changed the urgency. Now more than ever, I had to complete this job. Even if it broke my heart in the process.

Because I had to face the truth: I was falling for Jack Bradley.

And the only gift I could give him was a miracle with somebody else.

CHAPTER 12
Jack

Great job, Jack. You stopped physically driving Delia out of your life and switched to emotionally pushing her away. Way to double down.

My hands clenched around the steering wheel until my knuckles ached as I wheeled into a parking spot and slammed on the brakes. The truck was agonizingly quiet, and I had the urge to switch on the radio, but I wasn't sure I could handle any more Christmas music. A single jingle bell or a lyric about falling in love under the mistletoe would send me spinning back into a dark void.

Which was why showing up at the town's holiday festival was a terrible idea. There was zero chance of me getting out of this unscathed. But even knowing that, I still had to come. The festival was probably one of the last times I'd get to see Delia with a smile on her face.

Our paths hadn't crossed much the last couple of days on the farm. Mostly because I'd spent them hiding —*I mean cutting down trees*—in the field. Ironically, the business had picked up due to word getting out about the donated tree. Customers even paid full price, so I was riding that high, even though underneath it all, I was lower than low.

Christmas was next week, and Delia would be gone for good. My life had turned into an Advent calendar of misery, each door giving me a taste of something sweet, only to lead to the day that would hurt the most. Today was another one of those doors that I just had to open.

I climbed out of my truck and was instantly hit with a wave of merriment in the air. A gut punch all things considered. The streets were lined with people funneling into the town square and the bustling winter market. Every year, vendors set up booths selling homemade items and baked goods. Businesses hawked their wares and special holiday promotions. A band played and hot chocolate flowed like a velvety rich river.

The striking tree I'd cut and had delivered earlier in the week stood in the center of the square, already decked out with glittering balls and bows, and long swaths of lights, waiting for its grand moment.

"Jack!"

I tensed at hearing my name and spotted the mayor stepping down the platform steps. Becky's father was a gruff man with a trim beard and silver streaks in his hair. He wore a long black wool jacket with the town's emblem pinned to his chest.

"Mr. Mayor," I said, angling my head in greeting. Preparing for the worst, I folded my arms over my chest and squared my stance. Might as well get the backhanded comments out of the way so I could move on to the next stop on Jack's Tour of Misfortune.

The mayor's features drew together, and he smoothed the lapels of his jacket. He looked uncomfortable as if he wasn't sure how to start, and he stalled, waving to families as they passed.

"Look, Dad! It's the most beautiful tree I've ever seen," a little boy crooned, reaching out to touch the needles as his family huddled around the towering tree. I watched as they marveled over the size and took guesses at how many ornaments were used and how many strings of lights it took to reach the top.

They used to do that at the tree farm too in years past. Kids would rush through the fields, shouting in delight when they'd found the one for them. They'd watch in awe as we wrapped the tree in twine and attached it to the roof of their car, knowing presents would soon sit beneath those decorated branches.

The tension eased from my shoulders, and an incredible feeling expanded inside my chest. *Unbelievable...* Even though we hadn't been part of those families, we were soaking it all in. Just like Delia had said. Their joy had transferred to us and that had made what we were doing special.

Maybe that was why my dad had loved the farm so much.

Clearing his throat, the mayor turned his attention back to me. "Jack. I know this is a tough time of year for you and your family, and in recent times there's been a lot of conflict. But you did all right, helping us out this year, and that needs to be said."

The mayor extended his hand, and I hesitantly reached out to shake it. "Thanks, sir."

"If you're around next year, we'd like to do business again. Not a donation. This time we'll place an order in advance. Just speak with my assistant."

My mouth opened, but nothing came out. Could I make it another year? Did I want to? Those hadn't even been questions until recently. *No, and No. Don't bother asking.* But now? Maybe I should give it some thought.

"I'll let you know, sir. Thank you."

He clapped his hand on my back and then wandered off into the crowd. Almost in a daze, I followed the stream of people, walking under a huge festival banner, and into the holiday market. Grandma Jean and her ladies' club had a booth set up somewhere in the throng of vendors. That's where I'd find Delia, likely taking notes for her article while absorbing all the Christmas vibes. There was enough here to last all year.

I walked the edge of the market, stopping to peer at some of the items. Grandma Jean could use a new scarf, something navy blue with moons and stars would look nice, or maybe some scented candles. I'd have to come up with something and grab some of that silver wrapping paper. A bow would be good.

It had been ages since I'd bought any Christmas presents, and even if I did, where was I going to put them? Under the bare tree in the common room? Next to the mantle void of stockings? A laugh formed in my throat. I really was a Scrooge.

"Excuse, me." A little girl tugged on the sleeve of my coat. "This is for you."

I stared down at her as she passed me a candy cane with a slip of paper tied to the end. After she scurried off into the crowd, I removed the paper and read the note.

Check your pocket.

My brow wrinkled as I patted down the sides of my coat. There was something thin and square inside my pocket, which was odd since there hadn't been anything there when I left the inn. Kind of like how there hadn't been a heart in my cappuccino foam or snow in the forecast the day we went tree hunting, yet we got six inches.

Must be magic. Grandma Jean's go-to saying whispered in my mind. I was starting to believe it.

I removed the box from my pocket. It was about the size of a coaster and tied with a red bow. Lifting the lid, I pulled back the tissue paper to reveal a small tree ornament in the shape of a raccoon. Another slip of paper lay beneath the ornament, and I suppressed a grin at the slanted script.

They didn't have any opossums. Merry Christmas from the One Who Wouldn't Leave. P.S. Meet over by the hot chocolate stand. You're buying.

My gaze instantly snapped to the crowd as I searched for the hot chocolate stand. Where was that thing? I followed the green cardboard cups, spotting the line that wrapped around one of the booths. Was that a spring in my step? *Easy pal...* I forced myself to slow down, strolling casually toward the back of the line.

"Hey, Jack." Becky waved and held up a similar note-tied candy cane. "Let me guess, you got one of these as well?"

"What's going on? Where's Delia?" The line moved, and I looked over the tops of people's heads to find her. It had been way too long, and I craved seeing her candy cane striped scarf, her wicked grin, and eyes made of pure mischief. I hoped she was wearing her new boots.

"Wait. You seriously haven't noticed?" Becky unwrapped the plastic around her candy cane and stuck the curved end between her teeth.

"Noticed what?"

"The matchmaking. It seems Delia has gotten it in her head that you and I should be an item. I suspect Grandma Jean put her up to it or maybe Delia thought it would be a fun twist for her article. You know the Spells and Brews club are always hosting those mixers. Either way, it's pretty obvious."

Was that why Delia constantly pointed out Becky's qualities? I shook my head as I saw everything in a new light. "You didn't put a heart in my cappuccino foam, did you?"

"Nope! And I bet you didn't write me a cute note on a napkin with your phone number."

"I didn't. Did you leave a box of my favorite pastry on the front porch of the inn?"

Becky smirked. "I don't even know what your favorite pastry is."

My head was spinning. How had I missed it? Actually, that wasn't a hard question. I'd been so completely focused on Delia since she'd arrived, that the ground could have opened up in front of me, and I would have walked blindly into it. But it was time to set things straight. No more avoiding the subject or letting things go unsaid. If Delia wanted a twist for her article, she needed the right headline:

Lonely Tree Farmer Falls for Plucky Paranormal Writer.

"So what do we do now?" Becky asked as we worked

our way to the front of the line.

"I think we should go down the rabbit hole, and teach our meddlesome traveler a lesson."

"Oh, I like the way you think. Plus, it will be nice to have a little fun before I leave town tomorrow. Kind of like a last hurrah."

"Leave town? Where are you headed?"

Becky's eyes gleamed with excitement. "I was recently presented with an amazing opportunity. You know, Simon, Delia's photographer?"

"Yeah, I'm familiar," I said with a hint of loathing.

"Well, he not only freelances for the magazine, but he's an experienced food photographer with a job on one of the most-watched live amateur baking competitions. He took one look at my creations and thought I'd be a perfect contestant. It's already cast, but they fit me in. Filming starts in the city next week and they announce the winner on New Year's Day. I'm going to get to spend Christmas in the city!"

"That's incredible, Becky. Congratulations."

"Thanks. I think this could be my big break. It's what I've always wanted." She nudged me in the rib cage. "And Simon's kind of cute, don't you think? I like a man in a suit. Who knows what will happen once we start filming."

I laughed. "I thought you were supposed to be attracted to me?"

Becky lifted her shoulders and crunched on her candy cane. "I've always had a bit of a crush on you, ever since school. But we're not a good match. Besides, I'm pretty sure you have your eye on someone else, and I wholly approve. Be happy, Jack. You deserve it."

Strangely enough, maybe I did. I leaned against the drink counter and pulled out my wallet. "Two hot chocolates, please."

The vendor handed us our drinks, glanced at our candy canes, and informed us to check under the cups when we were finished. I rolled my eyes. Would Delia's schemes never cease? But maybe that's what I loved about her. She was eternally hopeful.

As we stepped out of line, I tipped my cardboard cup into Becky's. "To winning your first competition."

Becky winked. "And to making Delia jealous."

I slung my arm over Becky's shoulder and wheeled her back into the crowd. *Cheers to that…*

CHAPTER 13

Delia

Where were they? I stood on my tiptoes peering over the crowd, but I still didn't see Jack and Becky. They should have been here by now. It had been at least an hour since the little girl handed off the candy. Jack should have found his gift, and then off to the hot chocolate stand. That's where my little romantic treasure hunt started, all leading to the mistletoe arch we built next to the Spells and Brews booth.

The arch had been getting business all morning, bringing in the couples and hopefuls alike. It was beautiful with garlands and ribbon winding down the sides, and a single ball of mistletoe hanging from the center. Simon had been assigned to take couples' photos, and he'd grumbled about it, but it gave him a chance to use his new camera. All that was missing was our blasted twosome.

A sick feeling churned my stomach. Had they wandered off to be alone? Maybe the arch wasn't even necessary, and it was just a fun torture device for me to stand next to all day. The last thing I wanted was to witness Jack and Becky kiss. It was going to devastate me. But it was part of the job, and I refused to fail. The promotion didn't even matter anymore, I just wanted Jack to be happy. I wanted him to have a magical Christmas. If I got fired, so be it.

"Are you okay, dear? You look a little green." Grandma Jean set down her jingle bell bracelet and pressed the back of her hand against my forehead.

"I'm fine!" My high-pitched assurance said otherwise. "I'm just excited that today is finally here."

Grandma Jean frowned. "I know you're confident dear, but I don't think this plan is going to work. Mind you, this isn't a slight on your skills. I've been impressed with your dedication, but you must realize what's going on here. All the changes in Jack over the last few weeks have not been because of Becky. They're because of you."

Her words made tears pool under my eyes, and I wiped furiously at my lashes. "I don't know what else to do, Grandma Jean. This is why I'm here. I can't even remember an instance where the agency got the information in the file wrong. What if I follow my heart and make things so much worse? Simon said there are always consequences."

"Oh, forget what some foolish case file says! Life is never that black and white. Rules were made to be broken. Follow whatever phrase you like and just cancel this whole thing. I'll even rescind my letter to the agency. Case closed."

Could it be that simple? If I just ignored my job and went after what I wanted, would everything work out in the end? The crowd parted slightly, and I finally caught sight of Becky and Jack. My heart squeezed like a fist. Jack had his arm wrapped around Becky, holding her close, and they were laughing together, their heads bent like two conspirators.

Grandma Jean spotted them too, and her sharp inhale confirmed my fears. Somehow, I'd actually done it. Which should have been cause for a career pat on the back, but instead, it broke my heart.

"I sense black magic," Grandma Jean spat. "This festival is cursed. Where's my sage stick?"

I choked back a sob mixed with a laugh and forced a smile on my face. "It's not a curse. I'm just wicked good at my job. Maybe too good," I mumbled. "They should promote me to CEO."

"You're not *that* good." Grandma Jean stalked toward the booth, snatching up her jingle bells with a curse.

Clearly, I was. Jack leaned down to whisper something in Becky's ear, and she lifted her hand to touch his cheek.

She. Touched. His. Cheek.

The move made me want to snap a candy cane and file it into a shiv. But that wasn't very professional. I should just use a regular stick. Nothing holiday-related. They'd never tie the crime back to me.

The pair moved closer to the mistletoe arch which was empty and calling to the new couple like a siren on a rock. *Why did I make it so beautiful?* I was standing right next to the arch. Garland was literally in my face. Could they not see me or were they so blinded by attraction that I might as well have been a fire hydrant? Simon waved them under the arch with fake enthusiasm and lifted his camera.

My head exploded.

I'm not watching this. I whirled and dove for a secluded spot. Anywhere I didn't have to see the effects of mistletoe or hear the crowd cheer from another kiss.

A hand grabbed me around the wrist before I'd made it a few feet.

"Going somewhere, Delia?"

I froze, my feet stumbling to a halt. *These boots really do have great traction.* I closed my eyes and prepared myself for an uncomfortable confrontation. The pep talk in my head went something like this:

All you wanted for Christmas was Jack's happiness. Put down the metaphorically razor-edged candy cane.

My teeth ached from the sweetest in my voice. "Jack, you came to the festival. I'm so pleased. Did you find my gift?"

"I did. I'll treasure it always."

"Ha. In a box collecting dust with the rest of the ornaments?" I asked dryly, twisting my arm out of his hold and brushing past him, searching for the quickest way out.

"Oh no. I'm planning on having someone over for Christmas. I'll need to decorate. Wouldn't want them to think I'm a monster."

"Well, good for you. I'm sure you and Becky will have a memorable time. Don't worry about me, I'll check out early and leave you a stellar review."

Now that I was turned around, the mistletoe arch was blocking my way. A fitting end to another unsuccessful year in the romance department. *Sure, make the jilted witch march through mistletoe alone in front of a crowd of onlookers and a booth full of my new spell-loving friends. Just peachy.*

"Delia?"

I wavered and faced Jack, surprised by the intensity of his gaze. Everyone around us had gone quiet, and I peered down at my feet wishing for a whiteout blizzard I could vanish into. Another few seconds of this unbearable silence and I was casting one.

"What is it?"

"I asked you once before, and I'll ask you again. Are you jealous?"

"Yes!" The word burst from my throat, and I threw up my hands in defeat. "Are you happy? Thanks to you, I considered committing a holiday homicide. I just couldn't decide if it would be a single or a double."

Jack's mouth hitched into a tempting grin, and he moved forward, forcing me back a few steps. "Good."

"Good? You want me to spend Christmas in a jail cell?" I angled my head back, my hands fisted on my hips.

"No. I want you to stand right where you are and hold still."

Hold still? My chin tilted up, gaze traveling to the ball of mistletoe suspended over my head. *Oh boy... Blizzard activate.* As the silence deepened, light snow fluttered softly to the ground. Jingle bells sounded, suspiciously like the ones Grandma Jean had been ringing.

Jack stepped under the arch, his hands coming up to cup the sides of my face. The snow fell faster, swirling around us. I blinked as it caught in my lashes. Brilliant hope rose inside my chest. This wasn't some magic spell I had control over, one I could bend to my will. This was an unruly, wild moment of anticipation.

When Jack's gaze dropped to my lips, I held my breath.

"Delia," he said with a rusty scrape in his voice. "I don't know where you got the idea, but you're a tinsel-obsessed troublemaker, and I don't want Becky. I never did. I only want you."

He lowered his lips to mine, sweeping softly at first, then pulled me closer, taking my mouth in a deep kiss. I would have sighed if I'd had any air left, or melted into a puddle like an icicle at the first hint of spring.

A roar of voices cheered us on, but I didn't pull away, only buried my fingers into the flannel shirt peeking from between his coat. *Move along folks, this arch is occupied.* And I was taking it back with me so I could install it outside my room at the inn. I was going to hold court under it.

I smiled against Jack's lips. "I guess I'm staying for Christmas."

With a discontented growl in the back of his throat, he brushed his mouth over mine again. "Just Christmas? Looks like I have my work cut out for me to make you stay longer."

CHAPTER 14
Delia
—Christmas Eve—

What a whirlwind of a week.

Thanks to the publicity of a Bradley Farm tree in the town square, and after Jack's very public, and very swoon-worthy display of affection, everyone was willing to give him a second chance, and all whispers of the past faded in the face of Jack's new friendly temperament. The tree farm had an eleventh-hour surge of success as people shopped for last-minute trees with promises to return next year, wreaths, and decorated garlands Grandma Jean and I rushed to put together.

I may have even used some magic to meet the quota, but that was my business. I wasn't about to spend night and day assembling branches when I could join Jack in the fields. By the end of the week, there wasn't a tree we hadn't slipped behind for a long, lingering kiss. Plus, I got pretty good at using the saw.

Simon and Becky had left town right after the festival, and I couldn't have been happier. Not only because I was rid of my once and only in my head romantic rival, but Becky was off to chase her dreams, and Simon was handling her case. If any agent could grant her a miracle, it would be him.

And just maybe, by the secret looks they had cast each other before they left, Becky might get two miracles for one. Lucky girl. I may have found love, but I hadn't followed agency rules, and it was unlikely I'd get a promotion. After the holiday, I'd have to head back to the office with my tail between my legs and report to my dreary cube next to Agatha for my punishment.

Though I had considered hanging my own shingle. I'd have to find my own clients and do all my own research. It would be a huge undertaking, but might be worth it to continue doing what I love.

There was also one more sticky situation. Jack still thought I wrote for a magazine, and discovering the reality about who I was and what I did for a living might be one magical truth too far. Grandma Jean promised me he'd understand and even accept who I was, but I was worried and had decided not to say anything until after Christmas.

Let him have one memorable Christmas before I potentially ruin everything. This was probably what Simon had meant about consequences. There was no guarantee our relationship would work out, though I wasn't planning to give up without a fight.

Heaving a sigh, I flipped the closed sign on the little stand of wreaths and set about putting away the last of our materials. It was Christmas Eve, and the town was finally settling down for the night to enjoy the holiday. But for Jack and I, there was still lots to do. With all the chaos over the last few days, the inn was still devoid of decorations. That was changing tonight.

Grandma Jean poked her head through the door of the wooden shelter and stepped inside, doing a little twirl to show off her stylish outfit. She wore a red silk blouse with a ruffled neckline and a pair of trim black pants. Silver chains jingled together around her neckline.

"Wow, Grandma Jean, you look great!"

"Thank you, dear. I'm off to meet the ladies from the club for a few holiday cordials. Are you sure you don't want to come? They'd love to have you."

"I would be there in a second, but I promised Jack I'd help get the decorations down from the attic, and I already sent him up there to make sure he clears out any wildlife before I arrive. But squirrels or no, we can't wake up tomorrow with the place looking like it is."

Grandma Jean laughed. "Good plan, and no, we can't! Well, then I will leave all the decorating to you."

"Don't worry. I won't let you down."

"I have faith in you, dear. I did from the moment you arrived. See you later tonight." She leaned in and gave me a tight hug, then with a cheery smile, she jangled her keys and bustled out the door to meet her friends.

As I walked back to the inn with the setting sun at my back, I took a deep breath of the fresh pine air and looked around. This was a wonderful place to spend Christmas, and after a lifetime of lonely Christmases, I was ready to spend one with a family.

Taking the steps two at a time, I made my way toward the attic staircase. Boxes shuffled over my head, and I heard a muffled curse echoing down the hall.

Balancing on the retractable stairs, I climbed into the attic and waved away the thick dust motes hanging in the air.

Jack stood in the corner, massive garlands and boxes of ornaments lay at his feet. He fumbled with a string of lights, cursing again at the knotted lengths that had somehow wrapped around his arms.

"How are you tangled up in Christmas lights?" I asked, humor threading through my voice.

"These are a scourge on Christmas and should be banned!" Jack grumbled, struggling out of the strings and dropping the whole mess onto the floor.

"They're just lights, Jack. They can't fight back."

"That's where you're wrong. They trick you by having one light out of a hundred on the strand blow out, and the next thing you know, you're snarled in their grasp desperately trying to find the right blub. It's a festive snare and you can't convince me otherwise."

Nudging the web of lights away with my foot, I wrapped my arms around Jack's neck and gazed up at him. "Looks like I couldn't charm all the Scrooge out of you, after all."

Jack's fingers sifted through my hair. "You love it when I'm surly. Don't pretend you don't."

Dipping his head, Jack grazed his lips over the curve of my chin, making me angle my neck so he could get closer. Then we were backing up, Jack pressing his body against mine. My boot came down on a bauble and the thin, glossy plastic cracked beneath my feet.

We both laughed as Jack scooped me up and set me on the edge of a storage cabinet. His hands glided up my thighs and settled around my waist as he claimed my mouth with a slow intoxicating kiss.

"We're never going to finish decorating the tree," I said, coming up for air.

"There's always next year." He kissed the tip of my nose. "Or the one after that." His lips found the pulse on my neck. "Or the one after that."

His words made my heart flutter and ache at the same time. *What if we only have this one Christmas?* I smoothed my hands over the stubble on his chin and held his searching gaze. I knew he was waiting for assurances. Promises that after the holiday, I'd stay. But I couldn't give them yet. Not until everything was out in the open, and I'd checked in with the agency.

"Let's just focus on this one for now. I'll help you tame those lights."

Jack groaned and grudgingly helped me down from the cabinet. We sorted through the ornaments and set the ones aside that we planned to use, then brought everything down to the common room. After stringing the lights and hanging most of the baubles, we stepped back and admired our work.

All that was left was illumination. Jack reached behind the tree and plugged in the lights, setting off a colorful display that bounced like prisms off the gleaming ornaments. He stood behind me, enfolding his arms around my shoulders. I leaned against him and nuzzled my head under his chin, locating my favorite ornament front and center. The little raccoon hung delicately from a branch, swaying gently, then settling into place.

"I'm keeping the farm," Jack said softly. "For a long time, I thought my dad loved this place more than me. But thanks to you, I don't believe that anymore. This farm is a part of people's lives and their traditions, and we get to be a part of that. I'd like to think he just wanted to share that with me, and even though neither of us went about it the right way, I realized maybe he was trying to give me a gift and not a burden."

I tilted my head to look up at him. "That's amazing Jack. I think he'd be happy to hear that."

"Yeah. I can't take back the things that were said or change the way things ended between us. But I can move forward by making new memories and honoring him that way. It'll be a lot of work to get everything back to the way it was, but I'll hire help, and we'll get there. And I was thinking…" Jack hesitated, and I had to nudge him in the side to continue.

"What were you thinking?"

"Next year, I want to do another toy drive to make up for the one we lost. It'll be bigger and better, and actually make it to the kids this time."

"I think that's a great idea, and I'd love to help you put it together." As the words left my mouth, I bit my tongue, but Jack chuckled in my ear.

"I'll remember you said that. But first, don't go anywhere. We forgot the box that contains the tree star. I'll go back and get it." Jack planted a kiss on my forehead, then jogged from the room and back up the stairs.

I shook my head. So much for not giving any assurances. Oh well, a little one couldn't hurt.

As I was gathering the empty boxes to bring back up to the attic, my phone chimed. I slipped the phone from my back pocket and noticed a text from Simon. We hadn't spoken since he'd left to finish his case, but I tapped his name to open the message.

A photo appeared of Jack and me underneath the mistletoe. Pinching my fingers, I zoomed in, grinning at the cherished moment captured in time. This must have been the photo Simon snapped at the festival. I hadn't realized he'd taken one.

Another text came through. This one was a short message followed by a link.

Simon: I'm sorry to do this. But I had to warn you when I found the correct passage. Maybe they'll make an exception. Take care, Frost. See you in the new year.

My finger hovered over the link, unease keeping me from clicking it. I knew whatever was on the other side of that link wasn't going to be good. With a deep breath, I gathered the courage and tapped the screen. A page from a document loaded, and I squinted at the tiny text in the corner revealing the page to be from our employee handbook.

Simon had highlighted a passage, and I skimmed through it. A horrifying numbness spread through my body as the words took hold. I blinked, desperate for the disturbing lines to disappear, but they remained in cold, steadfast pixels.

Section 375
Paragraph Four

Non-Completion of A Matchmaking Case File As Assigned by Management

Agent shall follow instructions and data provided in the case file, and shall not deviate or change data without prior authorization in writing. If the agent fails to complete the case file as directly assigned, the agent shall forfeit all future duties relating to the client. To protect client confidentiality and agency assets, the client will lose all memory of any agent or agent activity beginning at the designated deadline documented in the case file.

The client will continue their existence as if the agent had not intervened. All traces of the agent shall vanish, and all associates of the client will lose any knowledge of the agent or agent activity. This decision is final.

My phone clattered to the floor as my heart roared in my ears. Technical though it may be, the meaning was simple. Because I'd failed to complete the case file as written, at midnight tonight, Jack was going to forget I existed. He'd wake up Christmas morning still hating Christmas and at odds with the town and the memory of his father.

This was my fault. How could I be so reckless as to not read the fine print? Panic seared through my chest. I couldn't let this happen. It wasn't fair. Not when Jack had changed for the better and had healed. To take all that away now was unimaginably cruel. Even if we couldn't be together, and I had to accept the punishment alone, I needed to stop Jack's memories from being erased.

I dropped to the floor and grabbed my phone, swiping through the lock screen. It was Christmas Eve, the night of the our annual employee holiday party. The office would be filled till midnight with top executives. Someone there had to have the power to reverse this decision. It was my only chance.

If I left right now, I might make it by midnight. With trembling fingers, I dialed a taxi, then raced to my room to grab my coat and purse. Jack was coming down the stairs, box in hand as I thrust my arms through my jacket and slammed a hat on my head. My boots were next, and I hopped frantically on each foot to slip them on.

"Delia? What's wrong?"

"I have to leave. Right now. There's an emergency that came up at work."

Jack's features furrowed with confusion. "But it's Christmas Eve, and it's already getting late."

"I know, and I wish I had time to explain everything. I really do." I backed down the hall, trying not to hyperventilate as Jack dropped the box and followed.

"Delia, don't go. Is this about the toy drive? I shouldn't have pressured you. Forget I said anything."

"It's not that."

"Then whatever this is, we'll fix it. Just stay here with me, tonight."

"I can't fix this from here!" Anxiety made my voice shrill, and I forced myself to keep calm. "You have to trust me. Trust that I'll make it right and that I'm so sorry. I never wanted to hurt you."

"Delia, you're scaring me. Wait, a minute."

Outside, the taxi had arrived, and the driver beeped the horn. Leaving everything behind but my purse, I ran through the front door and down the snow-covered drive. Jack was close behind, and as I whipped open the car door, he slammed it closed, breathing heavily.

"Talk to me, please. Just don't—"

Going up on my toes, I pulled Jack to me, breathing him in before I kissed him. Second, by second slipped away, and I didn't want to let go, but I made my fingers curl into fists and stepped back.

"If you wake up tomorrow, and I'm not there—" My voice broke, but I cleared my throat and pushed through. "Know that I did everything I could to make it back and that I love you."

"Delia—"

I pushed away from Jack and wrenched open the car door. Diving inside, I pulled it closed before I changed my mind and hit the lock. I rapped on the seat in front of me.

"Please, go. Now."

Jack pounded on the window, and a sob burst from my throat.

"Just drive!"

The car jerked forward, sliding on the slippery gravel. It gained traction and shot forward, leaving Jack standing alone in the driveway, shouting my name.

CHAPTER 15
Delia

"What do you mean there's car trouble?" I leaned forward and gripped the handrest inside the taxi as the driver pulled over to the side of the road and stepped out. He lifted the hood and smoke poured from the engine. I clambered out of the car, nearly slipping on the icy road, and peered into the hazy abyss that was the vehicle's inner workings.

"What's wrong with it?" I asked.

"I don't know. I just drive the thing. Don't worry, I'll call it in and get someone else out here."

There wasn't time for that! I hovered my hands over the blazing engine, hoping some magical energy would call out to me. If I knew which part to fix, I could use a spell, but I wasn't a mechanic. It all looked like twisted metal to me. Minutes were ticking by, and I needed to make it to the train station.

"Sorry about the trouble. I bet you're trying to get home for Christmas. It might be a while, but we'll get you back on track. Why don't you wait inside the car? It's freezing out here."

We were in the middle of nowhere, without access to alternate transportation. There wasn't even a house in sight or a parked car I could zap to life and commandeer in the name of saving Christmas. I shivered and slipped back into the taxi.

Reaching for my phone, I tried to dial the agency's main line, but no one answered. Not that I expected the receptionist to be manning her desk during a party, but it would have been nice. Next, I tried Agatha, cringing when I got her perky voicemail. I considered leaving a snarky one-liner but changed my mind.

It was hopeless. There was no way I was getting anyone on the phone. I had to be there in person. Which would be a whole lot easier if the car was running! I pressed the heels of my hands into my eyes, but the darkness only made it easier to visualize Jack's tormented features.

I hated leaving like that, but sitting Jack down to explain that I was a witch sent to grant him a Christmas miracle, except I'd messed up, and now he was about to lose all his memories from the past three weeks, was not a ten-minute conversation. Besides, if I failed to reverse the rule, he wouldn't remember any of it, anyway.

An hour passed while I waited inside the car imagining every horrible scenario. Jack called four times before I turned off my phone. Snow flurries fluttered in the air, making it seem like I was trapped inside a snow globe that someone had shaken and then perched on a shelf.

Finally, another taxi showed up to take me to the train station. As soon as the car braked, I jumped out of the taxi and ran to one of the self-serve ticket kiosks.

Bouncing on my heels, I swiped through the screens. When I got to the end, I tapped the print button and waited. Nothing happened.

My eyes crossed as I hit the side of the machine with my hand like it was a vending machine and my chips were stuck. The move rarely freed the chips, and it did nothing to print my ticket.

I glanced at the manned ticket booth, but it was empty and dark. This was unbelievable. Somehow, I'd found myself in the plot of one of those movies where the universe and everything in it conspired to make you late. Closing my eyes, I pushed a wave of energy into the kiosk, hoping I wouldn't scramble the thing permanently. It buzzed as the ticket printed and popped out into my hand.

Relief spread down to my toes as I raced toward the boarding train and claimed my seat. The snow had picked up, falling thick and fast outside my window, blinding the scenery as it rushed past. It made travel difficult, and by the time I rounded the corner in front of my towering office building, it was almost midnight.

"Hello? Is anyone there?" The doors were locked, and thanks to our security system, not even magic could penetrate the deadbolts. I pounded on the glass, seeing lights inside the reception area. Hope made me dizzy. They were still inside, and I'd made it in time.

A shadow bounced against the wall, and a man in uniform pushing a mop bucket stepped into view. He approached the door and gave me a curious smile.

"Can I help you?" he asked through the door.

"Yes. I work here, and I'm late for the party. Can you

let me in?" I searched through my purse and flashed him my employee badge.

The man frowned and dread doused some of my hope. "I'm sorry, but the party was canceled because of the snow. I'm sure they will reschedule."

"What?" My whole body seemed to collapse inward, and my arms dropped to my sides. There was no party. No one inside to help me reverse the spell that would take Jack's memories.

"Are you okay? Do you need me to call for a ride?" The man asked, but I waved him away and walked away from the building. I shuffled through the snow for a few feet and sank onto a metal bench. A lamp post illuminated the furious flakes and the empty street as the clock ticked down to midnight.

Tears slid in hot streaks down the sides of my face, and I huddled inside my coat. It was Christmas morning, and I was alone again. But this time, there was no joy to soak in, no family to sit with around the fire. Worst of all, Jack had lost his memories.

I'd ended up on the wrong side of a miracle, just like Simon had warned.

Fumbling for my phone, I pulled up Sage's number and hit the call button. The phone rang and rang, each tone sounding more miserable than the last.

"Hello, Delia? Is that you?"

I sniffed through the handset, nodding until I realized she couldn't see it. "Yes, it's me. I'm sorry. I know it's Christmas and you're still on your vacation, but I messed up, and I needed someone to talk to."

"Del, what happened? I thought everything was

going well. I got the report. Shouldn't you be celebrating your promotion? I was going to call and congratulate you, just not this early."

"There is no promotion. I ruined everything. I deviated from the case file and activated the client memory clause. I don't know what to do. I tried to stop it. I'm literally sitting outside the empty office building as we speak in the middle of a snowstorm."

The phone went quiet, and then Sage asked, "Del, didn't you get the memo?"

"What memo? Did I get fired?"

"No. Wait a second. Let me check my email."

Sage whispered something intelligible, then came back onto the line. "The memo's still sitting in my outbox. Technology was supposed to save us! But the service in these mountains is so spotty. Plus, there was the blizzard and the avalanche, and then I got distracted by Leo, my sexy former ski instructor who also happens to be the new owner of the local resort. Sidebar, if your hot as coal, Mr. Know-it-all ski guru tells you not to go down the black diamond slope, just listen. It'll save you a ton of trouble and—"

"Sage. What does the memo say?"

"Oh, right. So the thing is there was a mixup in the case file which is why Simon got sent out. Two files got merged and someone in the analysis department messed up big. Not naming names—cough, Tom— but Becky was never Jack's miracle. You were. It got messy because agents don't work their own cases, and if you remember, I was supposed to work the case originally. But then you were kind of nailing it, so upper management figured they'd let it roll, and sent Simon out to handle Becky's case. It's all in the memo."

"I was Jack's miracle?" I said, stunned.

"Yes, and the good news is they didn't wipe his memories. So maybe you could hightail it from the office and slip back in unnoticed to try and salvage Christmas?"

"Salvage Christmas?" I yelled into the phone. "I just traveled three hours into the city after completely ghosting Jack for no other reason than spotty mountain service!"

"You're getting a raise."

"What?"

"I just thought letting you know would help. Extra money in my pocket always helps me. Oh, and the office is yours, though I expect you'll be working remotely most of the year."

"Sage, I'm hanging up. I have to figure out what to do, and how I'm going to explain things. But—" My voice softened. "Merry Christmas, Sagey."

"Merry Christmas, Del. I'll see you soon. And boy do I have a story to tell you. Let's do New Year's at that restaurant downtown you like. Make it a table for four."

I smiled. "It's a date."

Ending the call, I stored my phone and wiped the snow from my jacket. I needed to head back to Wood Pine, and I had a few hours to figure out what I was going to say. But the worst had been avoided, Jack and I could be together, and I was definitely going to read the rest of that handbook.

With a lightness in my step, I turned toward the

train station.

"Delia?"

The sound of Jack's voice made me freeze in the middle of the sidewalk. He was here? In the city? Jack walked through the falling snow toward me, pausing under the street lamp. Exhaustion lined his face, but there was something in his gaze, and it was so intense I wasn't sure if I was supposed to leap into his arms or in front of an oncoming taxi. Since the streets were empty, I was counting on the first one or we might be here a while.

"Jack, how did you find me?"

"Grandma Jean told me everything. All of it. How you're a witch she hired from the agency, and how you've been trying for weeks to set me up with Becky. She said you wanted to tell me the truth, but thought I'd react poorly. Do you know how many Delia Frosts there are in the city?"

I shook my head.

"Too many. It's a good thing I tried your office first, or I'd be spending Christmas searching the city for you. Nothing you did over the last few weeks changes anything. I'm the one who tried tooth and nail to push you away, and if you'd actually listened, I don't know where I'd be. Your job is eye-opening, but also inspiring, and we're going to have a serious talk about how you use your magic." Jack paused and stepped closer until there was no distance between us. His warm fingers brushed my face. "But the thing I can't get past is why you left?"

"I thought I ruined your life, and I needed to fix it.

Coming here was the only way, except the office was empty, and there was nothing I could do. I thought I failed."

"You didn't ruin my life, Delia. Far from it."

"I know that now, and in the end, the situation turned out to be the one where I had the power all along. It's a very frustrating plot point, all things considered, especially during a snowstorm."

Jack dragged me to him, wrapping his arms tightly around my body. We stood in the falling snow, holding each other in the stillness of the early morning. There were no decorations. No sweet scents in the air. It could have been any other day of the year, but it still felt like Christmas.

Pushing the hair out of my face, Jack pressed his forehead against mine. "Delia, you told me you loved me, then got in a taxi and drove away. I wasn't sure if I was ever going to see you again. I didn't think I was going to get the chance to say it back."

A brilliant smile spread across my lips. "Well, what are you waiting for, a Christmas miracle?"

"You're my miracle. I love you, Delia Frost."

"I love you, too, Jack. Merry Christmas."

Jack dipped his head, kissing the snowflakes from my cheeks and the corners of my lips before threading his fingers through my hair and capturing my mouth. I sank into his warmth, delirious with relief and joy so bright it could have rivaled the floodlights Jack had aimed through my window.

All the pranks and all the suffering had been worth it. Jack was worth it, and I'd finally received the best gift of all. As Jack tasted my lips once more, my phone chimed, and I groaned, gently pulling away, afraid to find another passage of legal jargon in my messages. But it was just an email.

From: Sage Bennett

To: Delia Frost

Subject: Important Memo - Case Closed

"I guess service cleared up in the mountains," I grumbled under my breath.

Jack gave me a questioning look, and I held out my hand. "Let's go home, and I'll tell you all about how a file merge in the analysis department saved Christmas."

His fingers interlaced with mine, and Jack tugged me against his side. "That seems kind of boring for a holiday story."

I laughed. "Wait till you read the handbook."

The End

**I hope you enjoyed Delia and Jack's story!
The magic continues with Sage in
Witching You Weren't Snowed In

BOOKS BY THIS AUTHOR

Spellbound After Midnight

Wolfish Charms

Stranded And Spellbound

Shatter The Dark

Edge Of Wonder

Made in United States
North Haven, CT
28 November 2024